Apocalypse Fruit Basket

T. Monroe

Laguna Beach, California, USA

Apocalypse Fruit Basket

Neorevolutionary Press

For information contact:
tmonroewriter@yahoo.com

ISBN: 1461028140

EAN-13: 978-1461028147

Printed in the United States of America

"We're all equally alone and trapped inside ourselves until that moment when a piece of poetry, music, or art allows that break-through… the moment of connection with other human beings we long for."

Also by T. Monroe:

NEEVA'S GIFT
THE COLLECTED POETRY OF T. MONROE

“Mogro ohshon Mahuma awana yogro.”

Contents

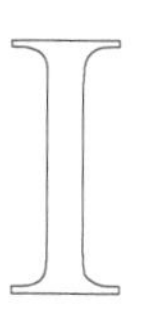

STRANGE FRUIT

John Silverthorne inhabited a rundown room meant for old bicycles, forgotten photo albums, and a grandmother's wedding dress. Sunlight forced its way through the dirty glass of the square window of a Laguna Beach attic. The owner of the two bedroom cottage house liked John well enough to let him stay in the attic. John liked the owner, Sam, well enough to accept his hospitality. Sam let John set up easels and work on paintings and whatever else he wanted to do in the attic, as long as John kept the house clean, did the yard work, and kept the house paint in order. It was a mutually satisfactory arrangement. John had found something of a patron in Sam, who knew some of the wealthier people in town. It was through Sam that John managed to sell an occasional painting to keep him in beer and cigarettes for a few months.

"Never sell a painting for less than $1500. If you do that, you're dead." Sam said when he took John in.

John blinked a few times as if testing the light with his eyes the way toes test swimming pool water. Satisfied, he sat up in bed and reached for his cigarettes. He shook the pack, opened it, and found two inhabitants inside.

"Shit."

He would have to go outside for more cigarettes, which meant he would have to get dressed. The morning was his favorite time to paint, and he liked to paint nude. If he had to go out into the world, the ritual was imperfect. He sighed and lit a cigarette, then pressed play on a small cassette player. A voice sang out pleasantly about driving a car into the ocean.

John walked around, naked and smoking, examining his three easels. One was a still life of various fruit, painted in dark and moody colors that evoked a sinister feeling. It seemed as if everyone in the world had died, leaving no one to eat the fruit.

He picked up a brush and added a mix of burnt sienna and other colors to the table leg. His cigarette had burnt down to the filter. Extinguishing it, he dipped his finger in the ashtray and rubbed the ashes over the stroke just applied. John cocked his head and smiled.

"Done."

John jammed the last cigarette in his mouth and crushed the empty box. He put on a pair of baggy green pants and pulled on a black turtleneck. Dumping the remains of a bottle of water over his head, he slicked back his chin length brown hair. The little tape player was screaming something unintelligible about

Cinderella. John found socks and his black boots, traversed the stairs and headed out into the street.

The Sunlight was much brighter outside. He always forgot his sunglasses and always regretted it. John paid little attention to his surroundings as he walked the familiar route to the gas station. He was almost there when he realized he had forgotten his wallet.

After walking all the way back to the house, he grabbed his sunglasses and started again. The street had many people window shopping and milling about. It was nearly tourist season.

At the gas station he checked his wallet. He was down to $20. That meant he better sell a painting. Otherwise he'd be shoplifting the paint he needed, and that always pissed off Sam.

"How are you today, my friend?" said the attendant.

"Good."

"Out of cigarettes?"

"Yeah."

"Good time to quit."

"Not today. Maybe tomorrow."

"You always say that."

"You always take my money."

He paid and took a pack of matches from the counter. Inhaling deeply, he walked slowly down the sidewalk admiring the ocean. Waves were high and the Sun brought out greens and blues with clouds of brown sand. John's stomach growled. He liked to eat at a pizza joint next to the ice cream shop.

"How are you, John?" said the owner.

John scratched his face. "Could use a shave, I guess."

"How is painting?"

"I just finished a still life of some fruit. I must have been in a dark mood, because it turned out spooky. Can I have a slice of veggie?"

"Yes."

John opened a can of soda and sat in his usual spot, where he could look out at the ocean. Out of habit, he went through a list of colors needed to create what he was watching.

Not that he would paint the sea. Enough people in Laguna were arrogant.

“Why you never paint the beach, John? I bet you sell more paintings.”

“Tourist Art. I leave that for the hacks. I’d rather put the feelings the sea inspires into my work. Why paint the corpse, when you’ve got the soul in a jar? Walk its circumference. Study it. Spread that sucker around. Paint the sea in every piece, just not in the obvious way. You might have to squint, but it’s there.”

John picked up the shaker of crushed garlic and poured it on heavy.

“You love the garlic, no?”

“Keeps the ladies away.”

“Lady trouble?”

“No lady, no trouble.”

The warm cheese and crunchy crust mixed with olives, green peppers, and tomatoes revitalized John’s sleepy limbs. The caffeine in the soda would probably make him edgy all day, but some days he liked edgy.

John continued watching the sea as he ate. Something about the ocean touched the hidden loneliness in him. He imagined his soul as a deep blue mystery. Besides, the sea made him feel less like breaking things. Somehow it understood him, and he it.

John went home and noticed the lawn needed mowing. He got the mower out of the garage and started on the side yard. Some friends of Sam’s walked by and waved. John shut the mower. He tried to put on a polite face, but he cared little for conversation with pretentious yuppies pretending to give a damn about art.

“How’s the painting?” one particularly irritating man said. He wore a sweater around the shoulders of his passionless polo shirt. John never understood why yuppie men always dressed like the 1980’s.

“Painting’s great.” John said unenthusiastically. “Sam’s not here. He’s probably working.”

"Jeff can really paint," the man continued.

"It's John."

"Oh, sorry." The man rolled his eyes at his companions.

John didn't want to talk to them anymore so he started the mower. It gave a good loud cough and roared to life. "I'll tell him you stopped by," John yelled.

He thought he could read the guy's lips say "artists" or something, as if he was excusing John's behavior. When their backs were turned, he gave them the finger.

After finishing with the lawn, John returned to the attic. He removed the still life from the easel and leaned it against the wall. John put a fresh canvas in its place and began painting three men walking down the sidewalk. He made the sky foreboding as if a flash flood would come any minute. The two figures flanking the man in the center had concerned expressions on their faces. The man in the middle was grinning. The sky just above his head showed the minutest break in the clouds, allowing a single subtle ray of Sun to illuminate the back of his head. The colors were just slightly more optimistic around him. John made the center man's bottom eyelids curve in a way that to the observant person would convey inner reflection.

John had been painting for hours, wholly engrossed, when Sam had crept up behind him.

"Very nice," said Sam.

"Jesus Christ, you startled me!"

"Sorry. I knocked on your door and it opened. Here, have a beer." John accepted the cold glass of thick dark beer. "I like this piece."

"Yeah? I just started it today. It's almost done. Guess I was inspired."

"What's it about?"

"Well, there's these three people, and the guy in the middle, he's in his own fucking world, even though he inhabits the same space as these other idiots."

"This is why I sell the paintings for you. The man on the left is the outer person weighed down by worldly cares, responsibilities, bills, etc. The one on the right is trying to live up to the image and expectation of society. The center figure is the inner person who inhabits the real dreams and desires of the man. It's in that world where he is truly free, and that's why he's grinning."

"Hey, you're the salesman. If people swallow that shit, that's fine with me." John laughed and punched Sam in the arm. "I finished this one, too." He pointed to the still life.

"Wow. John, it's very…sinister."

"I know."

"You are painting a lot of dark pieces lately. I think we need to get you laid. Which reminds me, I sold that piece you did of the cave in the canyon."

Sam held up a wad of cash. John swallowed a mouthful of beer.

"How much?"

"Three Grand."

John grinned.

"We're going to get you a show, buddy. Very soon, your own opening."

John took the money gratefully and lit a cigarette. He lifted his glass, "Cheers."

"Cheers," said Sam.

"How many pieces do I need for a show?"

"You should prepare at least ten."

"Ten? Shit."

"C'mon, buddy. You've been cranking them out lately. This is going to be your big break. You take that money and go buy the canvases and the paints and I'll sell another piece between now and then. But save these two for the show. These are your best yet. Now let's go get some dinner. I'll let you treat."

"Sam. Thanks." John smiled.

John and Sam cleaned up and walked downtown to a little restaurant that opened to the sidewalk. The people who had stopped by the house earlier saw Sam and waved.

"Oh, shit. Do we have to sit with them?"

"John, don't bite the hand that feeds you. Bruce is the one who bought your painting of the cave."

"Not because he appreciated it."

"Shhh."

"Hi, Bruce. Brenda. Julie. Do you all know John Silverthorne? He's an up and coming artist."

"We saw him earlier cutting your grass," said Brenda.

"Bitch." John said quietly through his teeth.

They sat down and John immediately ordered a pint. If he was going to have to tolerate the vapid, they would have to tolerate his drinking. Sam and Bruce talked about computers, which was Sam's business specialty. Julie pretended to follow their technical jargon about modems, soundcards, and ether ports. That left Brenda to strike up superficial conversation with John. After taking one look at her, he knew she was the kind of person who couldn't stand to be alone or ignored. He imagined she was always on the phone when at home and would be intolerable to live with. John answered her shallow banter with outlandish answers just to amuse himself.

"What does your family do, John?"

"My father works for the CIA. He's not really allowed to talk about his work. My mother is a tattoo artist. I guess she's where I got my artistic streak from. You ever think about getting a tattoo?"

"No, not really. Do you have any?"

"Only one. I don't like to talk about it, because it's in a really sensitive spot, if you know what I mean."

John hid his grin behind his beer. Brenda jumped at the pause in conversation to get on her cell phone. John imagined the radiation from the phone antenna creating a cloud around her head. He picked up a napkin and made a quick sketch of a skull surrounded by a radioactive cloud and holding a phone.

"What's that, John?" Asked Sam.

"Nothing."

He quickly shoved the napkin into his pocket.

“John has some great new work. I’m arranging a show for him in town.”

“How do you think it will go?” Bruce asked.

“I think this could be his big break.”

“That’s good news for my investment.”

“Investment?” John narrowed his eyes. Sam intervened.

“I--explained to Bruce, what a great investment art is.”

The waitress arrived with their food just in time to cut John off from saying something really nasty.

“Another pint please.”

“Make that two.”

“Sure,” said the waitress.

She was a pretty girl with striking eyes. John had noticed her before, but never had the nerve to speak up and say hello. He always left a good tip. Sam saw him watch her walk away.

“Her name’s Carrie.” Said Sam.

Bruce, Brenda, and Julie were engaged in a conversation about some television show they all watched.

“Why don’t you ask her out?”

“I don’t think so.”

“You’re not still carrying a torch for what’s her name?”

John swallowed hard.

“What if I am?”

“She’s married now, John. It’s time to move on. Admit defeat.”

“When denial is all you have, it’s hard to give up.”

Carrie brought two more pints. She cleared some plates and smiled at John. Sam elbowed him discreetly. John kicked Sam under the table. Carrie left to take another order.

“She smiled at you. Talk to her. What’s it going to hurt?”

“You know how it is in this town. Everyone drives a Benz or a BMW. They’re all out to show how much money they have. Old men picking up girls that could be their daughters. I don’t even own a car.”

Sam looked at John patiently.

"Why do you sell yourself short? You've got a talent most people will never have. That's worth more than a Benz. You can be charming too, in your less cynical moments. Take a chance."

"What if she's one more girl too scared to follow her heart, going to school majoring in Business Administration?"

"What are you two talking about over there?" Julie asked.

"The vapid," said John.

"The what?" asked Bruce.

"Do you know what vapid means?"

"Enlighten me."

"It means people with no balls, who never distinguish themselves from others in any meaningful way."

"Sounds dreadful. Julie, did you see that new movie?"

The three of them continued their light banter.

"I'm glad he didn't catch that was directed at him," said Sam.

"Whatever. I'm leaving. I've got paint getting old in its tube."

Sam grabbed John's arm.

"Ask her out. For your own good."

He was giving John the concerned friend look again.

"Okay, okay. This is stupid."

John chugged the rest of his pint and walked up to Carrie. She was talking with the hostess with her back turned. The hostess smiled at John and Carrie turned around.

"Hi."

"Hi. I'm John."

"Carrie."

"Nice to meet you. I wanted to ask you if you'd like to get dinner or a drink or something? Sometime? Not now. Because you're working and I just ate. But later. Not tonight though, I mean later in the week? If you're not busy? Do you eat dinner? 'cause we could just have drinks. If you drink?"

He felt the blood rushing to his face. Carrie thought his nervousness was cute.

"Sure." She scribbled her number on a napkin and handed it to John.

"I'm free Thursdays."

"Great. I'll call you."

"Bye."

John walked home thinking about Sam's way of pushing him into doing things for himself he wouldn't do otherwise. It was a rare thing in John's life to have a friend who was always giving without demands. Sam was more family to John than John's blood relations. He rarely spoke to them.

Inside the house, he went to the refrigerator and fixed a sandwich. There were plenty of pints left, so he grabbed one and headed up to the attic.

John lit several large candles, strategically placed to give just enough light to paint by. He pressed play on his little tape player. The canvas of the three men was almost done, but something was missing. John squeezed and mixed paint and in quick subtle strokes, created a small rat running along the gutter. Few people noticed the rats that inhabited the bushes in Laguna. It was the artist's job to give the subtleties expression.

The candles were making strange continents at their bases. Pools of wax spread and hardened slowly into green and yellow hands with melty digits.

John rinsed his brushes and put the candles out by pinching the flames between his index finger and thumb. He lay down on his bed, exhaling smoke slowly through his nose. The light of the Moon gave a gentle illumination to part of the attic. John played with the shades of blacks, whites, and grays in his mind until his cigarette burnt down to the filter. He extinguished it and fell into a dream.

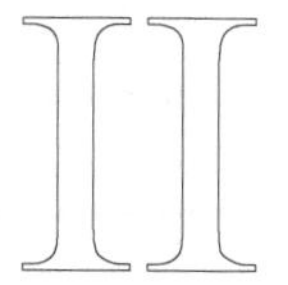

THE DATE

John paced the room looking in drawers and under books, behind canvases. He had misplaced his cigarette lighter the night before. His hand flailed over and caught the corner of the dresser in the center of his palm.

"Ahhh!"

He sucked his hand for a minute, and then carefully, slowly, probed the dresser top and finally found his fire. Ignition.

John backed up, exhaled and hit play on his little radio. Chaos erupted from the little speakers. He removed another completed canvas, and replaced it. John began painting a cluster of dandelions in various stages of life. Some yellow, some white, and a few buds. He paid special attention to the leaves, remembering how his grandfather would pick them and put them in their dinner salad. The light was playful, cheerful, and bright. John didn't realize he was humming a song that didn't match his usual tape. His eyes had darted a few times to the dresser top where a small napkin curled its corners like inviting fingers.

John walked over to the tape player and shut it. He picked up the napkin and started for the downstairs phone, then realized he was naked. That wouldn't mix with the large living room window and the neighbors. He stood in the hallway deliberating putting on clothes, went back into his room for a cigarette, then marched past the window unabashed.

The cordless lay lifeless next to the toaster. It hadn't worked in weeks. Like most men will, Sam and John had enthusiastically set about dismantling the device, confident they would soon discover the problem and fix it. They had just as quickly lost interest but were unwilling to admit defeat. The temporary fix was an antique phone with a wheel dial and a long curly cord. The sky blue of the apparatus clashed with the green and gold tones of Sam's house.

John smoothed out the wrinkled napkin and stared at the phone. He wasn't sure he could go through with the phone call. That would mean he would have to talk, and talking with strangers was hard for him. He dialed six of the seven numbers and hung up.

"Hi Carrie. It's John." He practiced it over and over. "Hi. Hello."

He varied pitch and delivery a hundred times. A thud on the front door signaled the delivery of the paper and reminded John he was naked. John began to wonder what clothes might be proper for a phone call of this nature, which led to other thoughts of other phone calls and clothing, until he was grinning to himself stupidly, naked in the kitchen.

John became seized with the urge to paint and trotted merrily up the stairs. Back in his room, he put a fresh canvas on and made the focal point of the piece a black phone. He quickly sketched a circle of people around it, wearing various clothing. He was smirking deeply when the phone rang.

All at once he was annoyed, hungry, and anxious remembering the phone call he still had to make. He let the machine get the call, while he worked with the undertones of his composition. A little nagging voice reminded him he had a million ways of procrastinating.

"Fine."

John raised both hands to the ceiling making the universal gesture of surrender to a more powerful force. He fished clothing from his drawers and resolved to face the phone demon down.

The phone rang once. The phone rang twice.

"Hello?" said a mirthful voice.

"Hi," John said, dropping the phone and scrambling to pick it up, "hello? Hello?"

"Hi. Who's this?"

"It's John. From the restaurant the other night. The guy-"

"I was wondering when you were going to call."

"You were? I'm sorry, I was just painting a little, and-"

"Painting what?"

"Ah, a picture of uh, people, uh making a phone call. Well different phone calls and they are all um, wearing different clothing. Clothing that is appropriate for each call," he gesticulated in a '*see what I mean?*' sort of way.

"You're an artist?"

"Yes."

"That's great. I've always wanted to paint, but my drawing isn't quite normal."

"Normal? Well, there's always abstract."

"I like paintings that speak to the soul. Do you like Georgia O'Keefe?"

"Yes. Love her. Great artist, great uh, biography. Really interesting-"

"John?"

"Yeah?"

"The answer is yes."

"The answer?"

"Yes, I'll go out with you tonight."

"Okay."

"My address is 1503 Daisy Lane. I'll be ready at 8. Bring me a drawing."

"Okay. A drawing?"

She hung up and John stood a little dazed. He was smiling, but it didn't go remotely like he'd expected. She had said to bring a drawing.

John got out his charcoal and a large sheet of drawing paper and sat down at the kitchen table. He began to create a large voluptuous flower in a Georgia O'Keefe style, but with his own flavor. After about five minutes he was satisfied with the charcoal, but thought something so vivid should have vibrant colors. John's oil pastels gave him a nice blend of passionate reds and moody blues. It was a flower of rare beauty. He singed it, and decided to shower.

On his way to Daisy Lane, John hummed a little song and crunched down upon dried leaves with his boots, creating a sort of crackling beat. The Sun was mellow, the hot part of the day being over. The light coming through the trees was gentle yellow fuzz, the kind found on baby chickens. For a moment John realized how vivid the world was to him, since he began painting. He felt little pangs of sadness thinking about people who didn't experience life through eyes full of wonder.

As John reached 1503 Daisy Lane, he noticed two small trees in terracotta pots on either side of the front door. The house was a gray blue with a brick red door. John's eyes moved from the doorbell to the black metal knocker. He chose the knocker and hit it three times.

The door opened and a tall woman with extremely curly blonde hair smiled at John.

"Hi. Is this where Carrie lives?"

"Yes. Come in. I'm Jane, Carrie's roommate. We share the house."

John stepped into the house and noticed it was well kept, not overly decorated, and a black baby grand piano was the focal point of the main room.

"That's my baby."

"It's very nice."

"Carrie will be right down." Jane motioned to the top of the stairs. John admired the grain of the banister. "Do you want something to drink?"

"No thanks."

"Do you mind if I play?"

John shook his head. He watched the stairs with nervous anticipation. He held the drawing enclosed in his sketchpad and waited. He thought he recognized the piece Jane was playing. "What is that?"

"Pictures at an Exhibition. Mussorgsky."

Carrie appeared at the top of the stairs smiling brightly. Her hair was pinned back from her forehead, making her sparkling blue eyes the focal point of her pretty face. She wore a simple casual black dress.

John forgot his nervousness and stood up grinning.

"You look amazing," he said.

"Thank you. You look nice yourself."

John wore a new black turtleneck and black dress pants with new black boots.

"Where are we going?" Carrie asked.

"Do you like Mexican?"

"I've been known to have a weak spot for guacamole."

"Great."

"Can we walk there?"

"Absolutely."

"Bye, Jane. I'll be back."

Jane stopped playing. "You two be good. No shenanigans, Mr."

Carrie whispered in John's ear, "a little shenanigans would be okay."

They made small talk on the way to the restaurant about the weather and how nice Carrie's street was with its cottage style houses When they arrived, the usually crowded dining room was packed. John had thought to call ahead and their table was waiting.

"Two for Bosch," he told the hostess. "Hieronymous Bosch."

"Right this way, Mr. Bosch."

She led them to a table on the patio with a soft candle in the center. They sat down and sipped their waters. There were roses growing in little fenced areas.

After a few minutes, a waiter came and took the order for fajitas and cheese enchiladas. He brought two glasses and a bottle of Merlot in the meantime.

"So tell me what your dream is, John."

"My dream?"

"Do you know what you want?"

John felt his admiration for Carrie growing.

"My dream is to stop living off the breadcrumbs of the rich and become established as a respected artist. I have been selling my paintings for decent money, but I want to get to the next level. The thing is, an artist has to do what they do for themselves. You can't cater to an audience or you're nothing more than a dauber."

"A what?"

"A dauber. An unskilled lackey who paints anything to survive. I don't want to come off as cynical, but I don't much like the people who buy my paintings, the types of people who run galleries or the art world in general. You wouldn't believe the politics and the bullshit."

"I'd believe it. There's bullshit in any profession. But it must be worth it if it's your dream, right?"

"I guess so."

"Did you bring me a drawing?"

John had forgotten about the sketchbook on the chair next to him. He opened it and handed the drawing to Carrie.

"For you."

She looked at it with beaming eyes. "This is perfect for my project."

"Your project?"

"Let me tell you about my dream. I know you like Guinness, but have you tried many microbrews?"

"I've had a few."

"I make beer."

"You make beer?"

"I brew my own beer and I'm going to open a microbrewery restaurant right here in town. I'm going to call it the Georgia O'Keefe brewery. You see, it occurred to me while my dad was teaching me how to brew beer, that beer drinking has such a macho connotation. The bottles are so phallic. I can't look at a beer bottle without thinking of a big penis."

John laughed and choked on his wine.

"I think I won't be able to *not* think of that after tonight."

"My dad and I didn't always use bottles, sometimes we used jars. I asked myself if the phallic medium of beer drinking couldn't be turned into something feminine and beautiful. Georgia O'Keefe, whom I love, came to mind. I'm sure you know she painted these wonderful flowers that were very sensual and erotic in their resemblance to the female genitalia. I have taken the beer glass and improved it, so the mouth is the mouth of a flower, the petals of a yoni. From a psychological standpoint I wonder if the whole ritual of drinking beer, meeting people, and the mating game would be improved by a woman's touch. I mean, think about it. Macho guys drinking from penis-shaped bottles in the bar environment, versus a brewery with awesome artwork on the wall, people drinking my special brews from yoni shaped glasses…it could really take the nasty edge off." Carrie looked at John carefully trying to read his reaction.

"You're not putting me on?"

"I'm dead serious."

"Brilliant. I think it's fucking brilliant."

They unconsciously exchanged the look all people do when they've decided they would sleep together if the opportunity presented itself.

"Seriously, you should come back to my place and try some of my beer."

"Now?"

"Right now."

"This is the best date I've ever been on."

John paid the check and they walked excitedly back to Carrie's house. They talked about Georgia O'Keefe and the turbulence and passion of her life. The warm night was a window box for the seeds of dreams.

When they got back to Carrie's a note was waiting on the table from Jane. She wrote to say she was spending the night at her boyfriend's house.

Carrie opened the fridge and brought out four beautiful jars of beers of different shades. John's eyes traced the contours of the masterfully done glass. He noticed the dark timbre of the stout, color like a rich soulful voice. The raspberry was slightly pink and smelled sweet. Carrie held some kind of tool that resembled a bottle opener and a putty knife. In a few quick movements the tops were off the stout, the blonde, the raspberry, and red ale. She motioned for John to step closer to the counter.

"Assume the position," she said smiling.

"You're not going to frisk me, are you?"

"Maybe later. Right now try the raspberry. It's my favorite."

John sampled all the beers, one after the other. The raspberry had the spirit of a wild vine, the stout a steadfast strong flavor. John was surprised the blonde was pleasing despite his usual dislike for them.

"Carrie, they're great. You really know what you're doing. And these jars, is this how you're going to serve them?"

"Yep. My roommate Jane found a place to make them."

John turned over the now empty jar of raspberry admiring the ivy entwined handle and the petals around the mouth.

"I love drawing but I only recently bought some paints to just mess around with and color in the design for the front of the brewery. Want to see?"

"Bust it out."

"Bring the beer."

John grabbed the two remaining beers and followed Carrie upstairs to the master bedroom. It was neat and girly with several large Georgia O'Keefe prints on the walls. Next to a comfortable looking Queen sized bed was a desk with a drawing pad splayed open. The sketch was well done. A sign over the two-door opening said "Georgia O'Keefe Brewery and Eatery". Two pillars flanked the doors with honeysuckle vines wrapping around them. The rest of the front was composed of large windows revealing tables and a long bar. John could make out the doors to a kitchen and brewery tanks in the far left. A set of paints and couple of cheap brushes sat pristine next to the sketch.

"You can say no if you want, but I'd love it if you'd show my drawing some color." Carrie looked at him hopefully.

John took up one of the brushes and began to mix paint. He went instantly into John-world, dabbing and slashing. It wasn't as satisfying as painting nude, but he pushed his sleeves back beyond his elbows. Carrie watched, intrigued with his focus. She brought more beer and they must have polished off four more jars by the time John finished.

"What do you think?"

"It's beautiful, John."

"Colors are like musical notes to me. Composition is sort of like, making a song. When the colors don't work well together or the tones contrast too drastically, it's like discordant notes."

"My father would like you, John. He used to tell me everything in the world is in motion because of the atoms constantly moving, and everything moving makes a sound. He would say 'Life is a big beautiful song, Carrie'. He would get all quiet after he said that like he was listening, like he could hear it. And I would listen really hard and we would sit together, just listening."

Carrie had been leaning over John looking at the sketch. Their faces were only inches apart. In the quiet of the moment John could feel his heart beating fast, and Carrie's heart against his shoulder blade. He wondered what music those two muscles were adding to the song, all the while staring into Carrie's eyes. She pressed her hand down on the paint pallet and ran her fingers along one of John's exposed forearms, leaving a green trail. Then she added red, then blue. She brought a smear of purple to his cheek and stroked his face gently. He brought his hands to either side of her face and kissed her slowly. Drawing his hands away, he smeared red and blue up her slender arms. Kissing and smearing paint all over each other, they toppled onto the bed. After wine and beer, John's world was fuzzy and warm, and with Carrie pressed against him, it smelled really damn good, too.

THE MANY TEETH OF GOD

Arguably the supreme product of evolution,
crocodiles have been around since the time of dinosaurs.
The Egyptians worshipped them as gods.
As man becomes more like the crocodile,
the chances of his continued survival increase,
and like the crocodile,
humans eat their young;
or at least their futures,
their resources,
water tables,
and ecologies.
One day we may become perfect and actually eat
their flesh,
sending our babies into an insatiable belly,
past the many teeth of God.

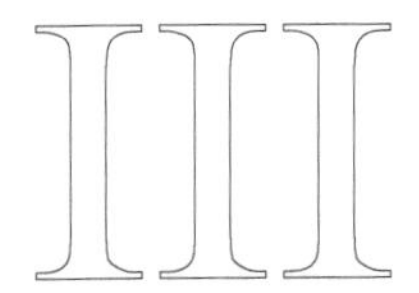

THE SHOW

"I didn't expect to see you up so early, with clothes on no less, and looking oh so nice." Sam had taken the handset apart again. He looked at John with an amused smile.

"Carrie's coming over and we're going to get breakfast."

"Ah. That explains it."

"What?"

"You being up and dressed so early. And not smoking like a chimney, I see."

"I'm trying to quit."

Sam stopped tinkering with the phone and looked at John thoughtfully, "You really like this one."

John was fidgeting near the calendar, noting the remaining days before his show. "She's different. Not like anyone I've known."

"Good for you, John. If you're happy, that's all that matters to me."

The doorbell rang. Sam yelled towards the door, "Come in!"

Carrie sauntered in and found John and Sam in the kitchen. "Hi," she said.

"Hi. This is Sam."

"Hi, Sam," They shook hands. "What are you doing?"

"Trying to fix this damn thing. I can't figure it out," Sam held up the phone feebly.

"Let me see," Carrie examined the phone carefully. "It's broken," She scooped up the parts, opened the trashcan and dropped it in.

"Um. Thanks."

"Are you ready, John? I'm starving."

"Okay."

"It was nice to meet you, Carrie. I'll let you know if anything else breaks."

They both admired the ocean as they walked up Pacific Coast Highway, past a coffee shop, and up a hill. At the top of the hill was a quaint little restaurant, unassuming in appearance but excellent in its breakfast offerings. The outside of the building was white; inside it had a log cabin feel.

John was torn between the French toast and an omelet. Carrie immediately decided on a waffle. The waiter brought them water and took their order.

"I like the way you know what you want, and you just go for it," John said sipping his water.

"I used to be afraid of mistakes, but my friend gave me some great advice."

"What was that?"

"She said: God damn it, Carrie, quit worrying about your choices and make some. You're going to make mistakes and pay the consequences. You'll see it's not the end of the world to fuck up once in a while."

"Hmm. Good advice. If fucking up was the end of the world, it's a place I've been far too often."

"So, why don't you have a car John?"

"I don't like to drive. What I would like is a car that you put the address into and it drives itself."

"How would that work?"

"I figure they have those global positioning satellites that can tell wherever you are at any time. How hard would it be to plug those into a city grid? They know all the traffic signals, they keep cars from colliding, poof! No more accidents, road rage, or outrageous insurance rates. No more traffic school."

"I guess that could work."

"Of course there would be the negative economic impact. No accidents would mean fewer funerals, less flower sales, less hospital bills, painkillers, lawsuits, and physical therapy."

"Right."

"But I have a solution. A built in computer glitch once in a while to help thin the population and drum up a little business for the coffin makers."

"Almost Utopian, John."

The waiter brought their food.

"Can you pass the butter?" John asked. Carrie passed him the butter.

"Are you excited for your show?"

"Yeah, I suppose. Kind of dreading having to smile and play nice."

"Even if people are paying vast sums of money for your work?"

"Especially, then."

"I mentioned your show to my Dad and he said you should paint some Tuscan Landscapes."

John coughed and a small piece of toast shot out of his mouth. "Tuscan landscapes? I'd rather throw up on a canvas and call it art."

"What's wrong with Tuscan landscapes?" Carrie said defensively.

"That's the kind of art people hang up to match their sofa."

"I can see that. My Dad has a couple of them. I always thought they were nice."

A crimson heat spread over John's cheeks. He swallowed hard on some milk.

After breakfast, John returned to his painting. With the show only three days away, he had produced 25 paintings. John had been toying with a small piece he privately called "The Sad Orange".

It was a small canvas about 10" X 10" that had begun as a joke, but had become John's favorite. Something about the tones of the background mixed with the main tone of the focal piece. It was immediately a contrast and a compliment. Maybe it was a marriage of opposites, one of those rare instances when duality becomes the key to unity. It was a subtle melody John heard from the colors, one the average person would miss. John reflected on his lack of regard for what average people missed. It expressed a core yearning integral to John's personality, this strange piece of fruit.

"Very nice," Sam said.

"You son of a bitch. You're going to give me a heart attack."

"Here, buddy." Sam handed John a dark glass of thick savory beer.

"You're forgiven. For now."

"Are you getting nervous?"

"Nervous? Me? Let's say I'm bracing myself for what I see as a necessary evil."

"You're the artist, John. It's your prerogative to despise the need to sell your art. Nevertheless, unless you want to live with me for the rest of your life, you've got to seize the opportunity. All I ask is that you allow the possibility that there may be people at your show who will like your art for the right reasons."

"I'll try to be nice."

"Promise?"

"I promise. You got any cigarettes?"

Sam produced a pack from his pocket, then drew them away as John reached out. "I thought you quit."

"I'm quitting. I'm not quite there yet."

Sam gave him one and lit it. They both turned their attention back to the small painting of the orange. Sam and John sipped their beer in thoughtful silence.

"The things you can do with fruit."

"Yeah. It's such a versatile metaphor. Sometimes it symbolizes hopes, labor. Sometimes a meal you've brought upon yourself, but really don't want to eat."

"John, you can be quite the philosopher, when you're not busy being a bastard."

"I think a lot of the philosophers were bastards. Socrates was a drunk, Aristotle a misogynist. Pythagoras had that whole bean thing."

"Bean thing?"

"He forbade his students from eating beans. Hated them so much, the legend goes he let himself be caught and killed by a mob, rather than escape through a field of beans to safety."

"Well, how do you like them beans?" Sam quipped. "How's Carrie?"

"Fine. She wants me to meet her parents."

"Scary. The faucet is leaking in the bathtub."

"You want me to call her? Maybe she can throw the tub out the window."

John arranged his paintings along the walls. Sam helped him compare and contrast what would go well at the show, proximity wise. They had three walls to work with. The first piece on the left would be the three men walking down the street. The last piece on the right, last of the exhibit would be the small one of the orange. They built towards the center until there was one empty spot right in the middle.

"What do you want the central piece to be?" Sam asked.

"I don't know. I've got four left over here. What do you think?"

Sam examined the four remaining paintings. None of them seemed worthy of the central focus. He looked at the right and left walls puzzling.

"There's a piece missing."

"What piece?"

"What's that turned around one in the corner?" Sam pointed.

"Oh, that's the fruit basket."

"That's the best one, John."

"No."

"Yeah."

"No."

"Yes. That's the center piece." Sam picked it up and placed it in the center. "This is perfect. What are you calling it?"

John scratched his goatee. "How about, Apocalypse Fruit Basket?"

Sam stared at and through the painting. "That'll do her."

The rest of the afternoon, Sam made labels with titles and prices for John's paintings. He also cataloged the order they had decided on, so it could be reproduced at the gallery.

"I don't want to load the pressure on, but this show could start your career as a respected artist. I've called every number in my phone book, invited every important person I could think of, even some people I don't like anymore than you."

"I appreciate that," John said.

"Remember when I met you, you could barely feed yourself? Not to mention you were shoplifting paint and brushes. I've got to admit, I'm nervous for you. I feel like it's your first day of school, or like I'm giving you away at a wedding."

"Thanks, Pops."

"I can't think of anything else to do. The art will have to do the rest."

The day of the show, John and Sam carefully loaded the paintings into Sam's car and unloaded them into the gallery. It took two trips to deliver them all. A lady in her 40's with badly bleached blonde hair unlocked the door and let them in.

"Next time you should rent a truck, so we don't have to waste time," the lady at the gallery scowled.

"She's a peach," Sam remarked.

"What a sour puss. Probably hates her life. Why do people stick with jobs and relationships that make them miserable?" John asked.

"Security."

"Securely fucked."

When they were done hanging the paintings, the lady shooed them out and locked the door from the outside.

"I won't be working the show tonight. Lesley will let you in around 6 PM. Try to be on time."

"What a relief," John said.

On the way back to the house Sam rehearsed with John, the small speech Sam would give and the typical questions John might encounter.

"Let's go over this again. How long have you been painting? Who are your influences? How would you describe yourself as a painter? What place does art have in the world today?" Sam quizzed.

"I'm not interested in any of these questions, you know."

"I know that, John. But it goes with the gig."

"Can't I interrogate them instead? Why are you here? What does life mean to you? What have you done about it?"

Sam rolled his eyes and pulled into the driveway. The show would be catered, so they weren't supposed to eat.

Inside, John went straight to the refrigerator for a Guinness.

"Okay, now I'm nervous," he said opening a beer.

"That's normal," Sam said.

"I feel as much anxiety about my paintings selling as I do having them not sell."

"Even an unhappy routine provides consistency and feelings of security. I read that somewhere."

"Thanks, Freud. How much time do we have?"

"Two hours."

John went up to his room and sat on his bed, smoking and staring at the window. He thought about trying to paint, having one extra blank canvas, but he couldn't move. Extinguishing his smoke, he put on his favorite tape and lay down.

A man-sized pig with a sweater tied around its neck handed John a wad of cash and exhaled a cloud of smoke from the cigar in its mouth. John coughed as the pig smiled.

"What a great investment," the pig-man said.

The words echoed a thousand times, and John felt like he was falling. He felt himself shaking.

"John, it's time to go. We're running a little late." It was Sam shaking him awake. "You alright?"

"Yeah."

The scowling woman was just leaving as John and Sam entered the gallery. She shook her head before disappearing into the parking lot. There was already a throng inside, creating an indiscernible chatter that made John think of cicadas. There were easily over a hundred people steadily grazing several tables of wine, cheese, and dip. Their clothes were expensive, their dental work flawless.

John wondered whom the people were and if he was in the wrong place. The manager of the gallery spotted Sam and came sauntering over.

"Ah, fashionably late. No matter, 7 pieces have already sold. Just under 23 thousand and we just started."

"That's great," Sam said. "Let me introduce the artist. This is John."

"Pleasure to meet you, John. Next time we will do numbered prints."

"Prints?" John looked puzzled.

"You can sell more copies, and of different sizes. Plus the original goes up in value. I bet you sell almost every piece tonight, and then we'll both wish you'd made prints."

"Next time, we'll be sure to do that," Sam said.

"We have a seat for you at a table right this way." The manager led John back to a table where he could meet people and answer questions.

"Can I get you anything?"

"I'd kill for a dark beer right about now."

"How about a nice merlot?"

"If that's all you got, okay."

"I'm going to go talk you up and bring some people by to meet you," Sam said.

"Sweater people," John said under his breath. He started humming songs from 1980's movies.

When there was a break, Sam asked, "How are you holding up?"

"I feel like the nerdy girl in a John Hugh's movie. And the popular guy is condescending to take me to prom."

Sam cleared six empty wine glasses from John's table. John looked up with a grin.

"We better get you some food."

"Why? I'm just starting to enjoy myself. I'm Cinderella right now, at midnight, a pumpkin," he laughed.

"You look more like Gus Gus with all that cheese," Sam pointed to an untouched paper plate. "We've almost sold out. You just made a ton of cash."

"I know, I'm a real social climber. What am I doing here, aspiring to be the people I hate?"

"You're doing what artists have to do. Think of Michelangelo, Leonardo, Mozart. Artists and patrons go hand in hand."

"What about Hieronymus Bosch?"

"What about him?" Sam asked.

"Some people say he ate moldy bread with the same properties as LSD, and that's where his crazy bugs and demons came from. But some people say he was secretly a Cathar, mocking his Catholic patrons with symbolic satire. How's that for artist and patron?" John smiled.

"Where do you get your inspiration?" a lady with obvious breast implants asked John.

"I watch the old Lon Chaney movie of the Wolf Man a lot."

"Oh. How interesting."

"Laguna of course is an inspiration," Sam said, giving John a disapproving look. "Such a beautiful town," said the lady.

"The people here are very inspiring to me," John said, smiling maniacally.

"I bet. I better go find my friend."

Carrie came in to the turn of many heads. Her hair was up and she wore a sleeveless red dress. She crossed the room in a few quick strides and bent over the table, leaning close to John's ear.

"Tell me your night just got better."

"You know, it really did."

"Hi Sam."

"Hello, Carrie."

"Who's that guy with the crowd around him?" Carrie asked.

"Oh, hey, that's an agent I invited. Harold Zamensky. He also writes for a couple of the big magazines. Let's go say hi."

"It's a pleasure to meet you Mr. Zamensky," Sam said. "This is John Silverthorne."

John shook hands with Mr. Zamensky. He appeared to be in his 60's.

"This painting is a wonderful. The Apocalypse Fruit Basket," he read. "I suggest you do not part with it this evening. It would be my pleasure to make a few calls on its behalf."

"I would appreciate that."

"Here is my card. I will be in contact with you shortly."

The old man excused himself. John followed with his eyes and Sam clasped his shoulder.

"It's your night, John. Well done."

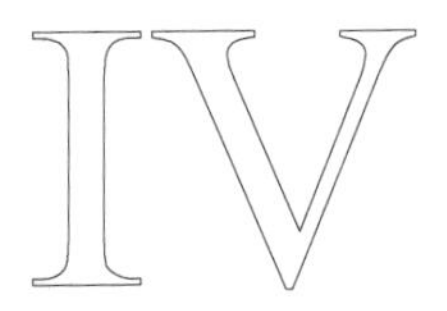

MEET THE PARENTS

John wasted no time getting back to painting. In one night he had made enough money to keep him in paints and canvas for several years. By the end of the week after his show, he had produced five bold new pieces.

Naked and smoking, John circled his five new works. In the early afternoon light, the attic seemed a chamber from his imagination, a place outside of normal reality. He knew the world waited outside, but it was the inner world that enthralled him. He walked around and around, stopping in front of a still drying piece. He didn't blink as Sam came up behind him.

A ballerina was dancing on a rope burning at both ends, her face wet with tears. The light pinks and grays of the sky could be taken as twilight or dawn.

"Is she crying because she's dancing alone, or because her dancing must end?" Sam asked.

John didn't answer. He turned the question over a few time.

"There is only so much time…only so much time to express everything you are. You, the moth, your passion the flame you must hurl yourself into. At the moment of ignition, a brief flash reveals your true being, and then you fade into the dark obscurity of time."

"I knew you were a philosopher."

"I am a moth, that's all."

"Hmm…I like it."

"By the way, Mr. Zamensky called and has sent an itinerary of openings, interviews, and estimates for getting your prints made. Looks like you don't need me anymore buddy. You art star, you."

John held up his middle finger.

"I wanted to ask you if you wanted to continue living here or if you were going to get your own place?"

"I hadn't thought about it."

"You're welcome to stay until I sell the house."

"You're selling? When did you decide this?"

"Seeing you become successful with your art has inspired me to do something I've always wanted to do."

John looked at him puzzled.

"I'm going to move to New York City."

"Wow. That's quite a change."

"It's what I've always wanted to do, and I already have some job offers."

"When is all this going to happen?"

"Maybe 6 months."

"I don't know what to say. I'm happy for you. I'll start looking for a place."

"Thanks, John. I'm going out to coffee, do you need anything?"

"No."

Sam left the house. The phone rang as soon as the door shut. John reluctantly left his sanctuary and went downstairs into the kitchen.

"Hello?"

"Hi, John."

"Hi, Carrie."

"I wanted to call and remind you to come over tonight at 6, and then we can drive to my parents house. They are excited to meet you."

John swallowed hard.

"Are you there?"

"Yeah, I'm here. Just thinking."

John fiddled with the phone cord and wished he had brought his cigarettes.

"How's your day?"

"Good, good. Sam just told me he's moving in the next 6 months to New York City."

"How exciting."

"Yeah."

"What's the matter?"

"Nothing."

"This is all happening a little fast for you, but don't worry. It's called the real world, John. You'll do fine in it."

"I know."

"Are you nervous about meeting my parents?"

John gulped again.

"No."

"They're going to love you. I've got to go. Be here at 6."

"Bye."

He hung up and sat down on the floor.

"I do not want to meet her parents," he said to the refrigerator.

"Hmmmmm," the refrigerator said. It just hummed along, consistently, never questioning it's allotted portion in life.

"What do your mother and father do, John?" he said in a mocking tone. "Drugs, alcohol, whatever they can get their hands on." He ran his hands through his hair, "No, I don't even know where they are or if they're alive."

"Who are you talking to?" Sam asked, returning. "I forgot my wallet."

"Myself. Carrie's parents."

"Oh."

"Other people have parents, emotional and financial support, college educations, and people they spend the holidays with. What am I going to say if they ask about mine? I've spent half my life with parents, and half living all over the country by my wits, wherever I could find a safe place to lay my head. How will they relate to that? I don't think I even want them to know."

"You are an artist, John." Sam put his hand on John's shoulder. "To produce great art, work that communicates the profound joy and sadness of the human condition, one has to go through periods of starvation, sleep deprivation, the worst living conditions imaginable, and overcome those states. That's the bio of most of the greats." Sam laughed, "You're in good company. Michelangelo rarely bathed, they say."

"Thanks, Sam. At least I have soap."

"Hey, maybe that's why so much modern art is crap. Because a bunch of rich kids with no life experience, no sense of life and death, heartbreak and awe, have become the painters, poets, and songwriters of the convenience generation. I had to work hard for my money, nothing was handed to me. Maybe, that's why I appreciate your art. I got to go."

John tried combing his hair different ways, and tried on a couple hats. At these times of intense self-reflection, he would think of her. The one who had taught his heart to feel again, then broken it. She was a brilliant poet, played the piano, and had grown up in the suburbs. John recalled their last conversation.

"I just don't know what I'm going to do with my life, John."

He had looked at her with disbelief.

"What's that look?"

"You are the best poet I know and you are talking about going back to school and finding a profession?"

"Poetry is never going to pay the bills."

John looked down at his feet.

"The life of an artist is hard. You have to suffer. You have to struggle. I wouldn't recommend it to anyone. Go to school. Play it safe. You're a smarter person than I am."

A year later she had married and soon had a kid. She was living the American dream. In John's mind, she had settled for a checkbook and a tract home. But he missed the hell out of her.

Carrie was the first person in years he had let his guard down for. He was hoping to avoid a repeat performance. John didn't know if a rootless gypsy was meant for the mundane security of family life.

6 O'clock came quickly and John was knocking at the door of Carrie's house on Daisy Lane. Carrie and John got in her car and drove inland. John found his mind wandering back and forth between the classical music on the radio and the urge to smoke. He didn't light up around Carrie anymore, but he more than made up for it when he wasn't with her.

They wended their way into the suburbs arriving at a private entrance and a large security gate. The guards recognized Carrie and waved them through. John couldn't fathom how people could justify paying close to a million dollars for a home. They went on throughout the rolling hills in a sort of maze that was the bane of food delivery people everywhere.

Carrie's parent's house was a large two story with very little side, front, or backyard, and with the same architecture as all the other houses on the street.

"The fucking American dream." John muttered.

"What?"

"I said I can't wait to eat."

Carrie led John in without knocking. The entryway opened to a large room with an extremely high ceiling.

"Hello?" Carrie called.

"Come in."

Carrie's mom walked out from the kitchen area. She was a thin woman with the short style haircut most suburban women eventually succumb to when they decide it's time to be *mature.* The endless tinting and highlighting is the life left for hair that will never again blow freely in the breeze. John thought of a few lines from a poem:

Do you remember the wind whipping our vagabond hair

In our laughing faces as we lapped rain from the sky

How quickly we fall into maturity's snare

How quickly youth does die

"Hello, you must be John."

"Hi."

John offered his hand, which she clasped warmly.

"We're almost ready for dinner. My mom and dad will be here any minute."

"Grandma and Grandpa are coming?"

"You're dad is going to help them figure out how to work their new camera. They bought one of those nice ones you can print pictures on your computer with."

As if on cue, the doorbell rang. John did a double take as Carrie's grandparents came in. The grandmother looked just like her mom down to the haircut, only with gray hair and a wrinkled face. If he didn't know better, he would think it was the same person made up with stage makeup to appear old.

Carrie's dad came in from the garage and greeted his in-laws, then John. He seemed a fit just under 50 man, with serious eyes. John could see Carrie's face was a well-balanced blend of her mom and dad's features.

"Carrie told me you make beer?" John asked.

"Oh, it's been years since I've dabbled with that old alchemy. Carrie's far better at it than I ever was."

As they sat down to eat, Carrie whispered in John's ear.

"Grandma likes her wine, and she always speaks her mind. A word to the wise."

John noticed the crucifix hanging on the wall behind Carrie's dad and a picture of the Virgin Mary on the opposite wall. He put two and two together and realized he had entered a Catholic household. Pope jokes were definitely out. He couldn't tell a joke to save his life, so he figured he was safe.

"We heard the most beautiful sermon today at mass." The grandma said. "I like our new priest so much better than Father Joseph."

Grandma sipped her wine. John sipped his. She eyed him from across the table.

"Is your young man a good Catholic, Carrie?"

"We haven't really talked about it."

Grandma took a bigger sip. John swallowed a mouthful.

"You're not a heathen, are you John?" She asked.

John smiled.

"Haven't heard that word in a long time. I wasn't really brought up with religion. I read the new testament once when they were handing them out at school."

Carrie's mom tried to change the subject.

"I'm getting sick of all the graffiti on the freeway. There was so much of it when I drove through L.A. today. I think those taggers should have their hands cut off. It's so ugly."

"Really?" John asked.

"It would teach them a lesson."

Three glasses of wine and John's general uneasiness with strangers was not a good combination. He hated religion. He hated religious hypocrisy even more. And he was still ruffled from the heathen comment.

"If Jesus came back today, do you think he'd be hanging out in Rancho Santa Margarita? Irvine? He'd be in the ghetto with the taggers."

Grandma looked shocked and disgusted.

"Those people aren't even Catholic. They're scum."

"C'mon. Jesus said he came as a physician to heal the sick. Not for the well. He wouldn't be living in a gated community, he'd be in the inner city with the gangsters and taggers."

Grandpa stood up with a stern look on his face.

"I'm going in the other room, before I start speaking German."

He left the room in a black cloud.

"Religion and politics are topics better left out of the dinner table." Carrie's dad said.

"So, John, Painting is going well for you?"

"Yes. Almost overnight my whole life is changing."

"What were you doing before?" Grandma asked.

"Living in an attic, painting, mowing the lawn."

"Sounds very Spartan." Carrie's dad offered.

"At least I don't have to shoplift paint anymore."

John chuckled.

That was the last straw for Grandma. She joined Grandpa in the other room. John downed his fourth glass of wine and excused himself to the bathroom.

"You're blowing it." He said to his reflection.

On the counter were little booklets full of articles written by church leaders.

"Jesus Christ."

The drive back to Carrie's was a silent one. John could tell she was irritated, but didn't want to fight about it. He had felt very little in common with her family, and frustration hung on him like wet clothing. At least they hadn't asked about his parents.

As they pulled into the driveway on Daisy Lane, Carrie finally spoke.

"That could've gone better."

John felt the cigarettes in his pocket like 20 little comrades waiting for the call to battle. He resisted.

"I'm sorry."

Carry leaned her head on the steering wheel.

"I know my Grandma is a difficult person. I'm not really into the church anymore, but they're my family. It's what they believe in."

"I have no problem with their religion. I just thought it was a little harsh. I've had some good friends that were taggers. Writers. I hopped trains once with my friend Andrew, and a lot of that is on the level of art. It takes skill, and care, and passion. There's an ideal behind it of personal freedom and expression."

"There are two kinds of people in this world, those who live deliberately, trying like hell to stamp a piece of themselves on this rock, and those who fall asleep inside themselves, going with the flow to maintain a sense of security and what society prescribes as the normal life. I have no place in that. It isn't me. I'd rather risk getting shot hopping a train, then spend my life on my knees, bowing down to icons and ideas that are 2,000 years old. All we have is now. Life is now. There's no safety, no security, no guarantee that you'll wake up tomorrow. I want to be that intense all the time."

"That's why you shut yourself in an attic?"

"Fuck this."

John turned his back and walked off, lighting a cigarette in clenched teeth.

"Run away!" Carrie shouted. "You can't hide form the world! I love you, you asshole!"

COLLISION

Collision, escape
moments of confused freedom
naked clutching stars

BURNING BRIDGES

Carrie had been crying for two weeks when she decided enough was enough. She dragged herself to the bathroom to survey the damage. Red eyes and nose from crying. Eye drops and some face lotion with aloe vera would mend those. Hair disheveled, tangled, snarled, and gnarled, resembling an abandoned bird's nest. Nothing a shampoo and a comb couldn't fix. She checked her breath. A toothbrush and some mouthwash would counteract that odd feeling coating her pallet and tongue from not eating for several days. Break-ups are often the most effective diets. Everything she saw and smelled was fixable. There was one more thing.

Carrie pulled off her shirt, and then unfastened her bra. She couldn't quite see it, but she stared into the mirror at the spot between her breasts. Under the flesh, blood, and bone lay the previously un-invaded country of her heart. But that time had passed. She was occupied now. If she was to know any peace at all, she would have to launch a desperate insurgency.

Carrie bathed, groomed, and sat down at her desk. The loan application for starting her business had been lying neglected under junk mail and bills. She cleared a space and put herself to work.

After finishing the application, Carrie picked out a nice skirt and blouse and fixed her makeup. She wore that particular shade of red lipstick that put all the attention on her pretty mouth. Taking a few deep breaths in front of the mirror, she practiced smiling. It was difficult at first, but she found visualizing the restaurant brewery full of people and bustling with life, it pushed out all other thoughts.

Walking through the doors of the bank, to ask for the money to pursue her dream, caused her to bite her lip ever so slightly. After waiting for 10 minutes, Carrie was seated at the desk of a professional looking man who looked about 40. He had a bright white smile that revealed meticulous dental care. He typed away on his computer checking her credit and asking numerous questions about equity and savings.

"Basically, Ms. Wright, when one opens a business, they are never sure how much money they are going to make. You say your father has a business and a great deal of personal equity, and you have a small savings. We're going to need your father to come in and fill out an application. We need to see equity, that you can budget for the payments, and we need at least 20% down on the loan right away."

"I understand."

"I've read your business plan, and want to ask if I was a tourist, what would make me choose your brewery over the others?"

Carrie smiled the way she had practiced, with calm self-confidence.

"Ambiance. A man will go to any old bar for a drink. My brewery is going to be an experience of culture and class. During the off season locals will come who love the atmosphere and the food."

The man looked impressed.

"It's refreshing to see such ambition in young people. I thought of opening a baseball card shop when I was your age."

He sighed.

"Of course I wouldn't have made as much money as my career in banking has made me."

Carrie faked a little laugh. She wanted to tell him it wasn't too late. That it's never too late to take a risk for your dreams, but she didn't want to offend him.

"When can you come in with your dad?"

"He usually golfs on Thursday, which is my day off. I'm sure he won't mind coming in after his morning round."

"Where does he golf?"

"Some place in Aliso Viejo."

"Oh, that's a nice course."

"Do you golf a lot?"

"Every Saturday."

"How nice."

Carrie stood up.

"It was nice to meet you. I'll see you Thursday."

"You bet."

Carrie's roommate was playing the piano when she returned home. Carrie sank into a chair and let the banking ordeal slide off of her. The music was beautiful and sad. She felt her mood changing. She tried to fight it, but she began to cry.

Jane stopped playing.

"What's wrong?"

"The music." Carried sobbed.

"Was it bad?"

"No, it was beautiful."

"It's Debussy. What's wrong?"

She sat down on Carrie's lap and put her arm around her.

"Shhh. It's okay. There's life after love. That guy's a big dumb jerk."

"I know. But he was my big jerk."

"Stop thinking about him. How'd it go at the bank?"

Carrie wiped her tears.

"Good. Really good. I need my Dad to come in and co-sign with me. I think if he just talks about golf we'll be fine."

"There you go. Hey I was supposed to go to a movie to-night, but why don't we just have a girls' night out?"

"I don't think I'm up to it."

"Nonsense. You get dressed up and we'll go out where you can see how many men ogle you. It'll make you feel better, I promise."

"You think so?"

"C'mon, get changed. We've got some drinking to do."

- - - - - - - -

John painted with a dark enthusiasm. His self-appointed agent kept him busy with shows and his prints were selling like dollar dances at the marriage of Helen. He worked at a furious pace, as if trying to prove something to the phantoms in his mind.

Carrie stopped calling after a couple of weeks with John refusing to reply. By the time a month had passed, John was deeply sorry. Instead of calling and making amends, he painted. He exorcised every demon in his consciousness, and there were many.

In one painting he called "The Beggars", a fat Pope led a pack of naked, emaciated men and women by the veins in their arms like a bundle of ropes. Their blood trickled into his gaping mouth. Another titled "The Pit" depicted an affluent man with an anguished look of one in the death throes of suffocation, as dollar bills stuffed his nostrils, ears, and mouth. He was sinking in a quagmire of coins.

Mr. Zamensky was brilliant at tying these works and others in the same humor to "Apocalypse Fruit Basket". In his newspaper column, in magazines, and on public radio he sang the praises of John's 'Post Modern Dark Romanticism'. According to Mr. Z., John was the leading painter in the new Dark Romantic movement.

John barely had time to pay attention to all his success. He only left the house grudgingly for the openings, and left the second his presence was no longer required, racing home in his new car to get back to the easels.

A good 9 months passed in this manner. John had moved into his own studio loft above a business in South Laguna. It was a discreet place where no one could disturb him. The only two people who knew where he lived were Sam and Mr. Z. He had furnished it only with a bed and refrigerator, a lamp, and a number of candles and candleholders.

One night, seized with the urge for Moonlight, he had drunkenly taken a hammer and started bashing a hole in the ceiling. He abandoned his impromptu skylight when plaster splinters had blinded him in both eyes. He spent a good hour in the bathroom sink, flushing and picking out the fragments.

Sam was more than a little worried about him. It was his last night before his final departure for New York City. He had found John's door ajar and John lying on the floor passed out. Empty beer bottles lined the walls, many of them overflowing with cigarettes.

"John. John, wake up."

"Mmhmph."

"John?"

John opened one eye.

"Hi Sam. Is it time for dinner?"

"It's 5 in the afternoon. Are you drunk?"

"Hmm. No. Just sleeping."

"Get up. My flight leaves at 10."

"Yeah, okay."

John stood a little shakily and ran coldwater over his head.

"You look like shit. When is the last time you shaved?"

John ran his hand across his face. He tried to look into the bathroom mirror, then remembered he had painted a big tree on it bearing worms, snakes, and scorpion fruit.

"Shit. I'm sorry man. I've been painting."

"I can see that. But you've got to take care of yourself. This place looks like a rat hole. I feel like I should be wearing a biohazard suit."

"Okay, okay. Give me a minute."

John put on some clean clothes and tied his unkempt hair back. It had grown considerably. Using the medicine cabinet for a mirror, he scraped a razor across his face to appease his friend. A handful of aspirin and a swallow from one of the open beer bottles, and he was ready to face the world.

"Where do you want to eat?"

"There's this new place downtown I thought we should check out."

"You want me to drive?"

"No, John. Once in your car was quite enough. I want to at least make it to dinner."

John laughed and clasped Sam's shoulder.

"You want to live forever?"

"No, but I wouldn't mind a moment of passionate ignition before I go."

John looked sad for a moment, then conceded.

"You drive."

Down town Sam led John past a building under construction and paused in front of a colored illustration of what the business was to look like when finished. It was Carrie's drawing colored in by John, taped to the inside of the window. John glanced over Sam's shoulder to see what he was looking at.

"Georgia O'Keefe Brewery" Sam read, "opening in March. Hey isn't that…"

"Yeah."

"Do you still…"

"No."

"What happened with you two?"

"I don't want to talk about it."

"That's a shame. You seemed so happy."

"Yeah, well, I didn't get along with her family."

"Did you give them a chance?"

John felt the blood rush to his face.

"A chance? Did my family give me a chance? Even when I was small, they were emotionally unavailable, alcoholics. Flying into rage at the smallest thing, I hated them for their physical abuse. The old man died when I was 14, just as we began to relate to each other as friends. My mother turned to cocaine, then crack. There was an entourage of parasites at my house, nightly. Siphoning her money and drugs. Sometimes I would come home from school and they'd all be at the dining room table, neat lines of coke chopped up on mirrors. Sometimes she'd be alone with the old man's urn, crying and digging through his ashes, screaming, "Where is he?" I was 14 and even the illusion of having a family, of being like other people if only in appearance, exploded in one single night with the old man's heart. There's nothing more chilling then coming home and seeing cars lining your driveway and street, and just knowing. What could I do but run away and keep running?"

"You can't run your whole life, John. Eventually, you have to face yourself."

"Are you speaking from experience? Have you ever had to face yourself?" John gave him a sarcastic look. "You've got holidays with the folks. You've never lived on the street. Eaten other people's garbage because you were hungry out of your mind. I'm sick of your self-righteous advice. Always trying to get me to be nice to people who value all the wrong things."

"And what do you value, John? Like it or not, you're a member of the human race. No better or worse than anybody else. You can feel sorry for yourself for the rest of your life, or you can choose to see the good in people."

"Go to Hell."

"No, John. You go to Hell."

Sam walked away, leaving John alone in front of the drawing of the brewery.

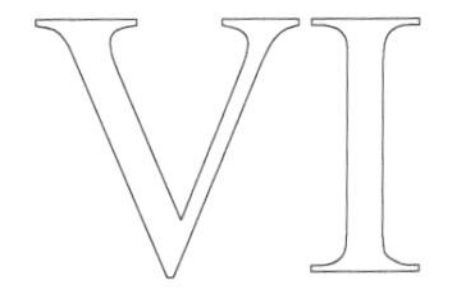

Meltdown

John languished in the double calamity of the ear piercing shriek of the alarm clock and the persistent ring of the phone. The answering machine clicked on with a chirp. A slightly brittle woman's voice reminded John not to be late for his showing in Newport Beach that night. John brought a shoe down on the alarm clock three times before it finally shut up.

The Monster, as he called the damn time-keeping device, was a gift from his agent, given after John was twice late for important interviews. He couldn't fathom why anyone in their right mind would want to wake up:

A. Before they actually felt rested.
B. To such hideous noise sure to produce a hostile disposition

John was planning the Monster's demise, but he wanted to make it look like an accident. It just wouldn't do to drop it out of his second story window unto the hungry asphalt parking lot below. There would be questions.

"How did it fall out your window?"

And excuses.

"I was setting the time, standing by the window, wondering if the Sun really was directly over head at noon, when a seagull flew by and startled me."

And crocodile tears.

"That was the best damn alarm clock anyone ever gave me. What a shame."

John's reverie was interrupted by more shrieking, and he realized he had only managed to bring the heel of the shoe down on the snooze button. If only he was a stiletto wearing cross-dresser, he could have put a stake through the Monster's heart.

"That's it."

John got up and gave the cord a tug, pulling the device from the wall. He marched slowly and solemnly into the kitchen, interring it in the oven. He stood there without turning it on, then cracked the door open slightly and peered in.

"Just you think about what you've done for a while."

John closed the oven door and thought of Sylvia Plath. He knew an alarm clock did not possess the quiet determination to stick itself in an oven, having tired of the thankless job of disturbing people's rest and setting them on edge. No. This monster would go on and on, confidence never shaken, unconcerned with whether or not God existed, or if an entropic fate awaited the universe.

The idea broke over John, how many people were like clocks. Unflinching in their routines, unshaken in their determination for steady certain monotony. These people resisted the changing nature of the universe to create their temporary, sanitary, and punctual ant-hovels. Only the hand of time, which never wore a watch, would wipe them and their clocks from memory.

John took to his canvases and quickly created the outline of two businessmen shaking hands. As the details filled in, their ties were blowing in the wind against a brown dust-storm sky. Instead of human heads, they had cuckoo clocks under their business suit hats. In a small corner, John added in a very small anthill where barely visible ants were constructing a sundial. He would call this piece "The Futility of Timekeeping".

The phone rang again, bringing John back to the need to get dressed and ready for the show in Newport Beach. The prints were ready; everything was efficiently handled for him. All he had to do was show up reasonably sober, smile, and nod. That was the hard part.

John looked around his place, letting his eyes linger on the new furniture, the vintage record player that played real vinyl, the solid oak bookshelves filled with brand new copies of thick books with the works of his favorite artists. His car keys sat on a coffee table, car manufacturer logo looking up at him like an accusation.

"Where did I get all this shit?"

He decided to have a beer before leaving. The shiny new refrigerator offered five kinds of dark and red beers, and not much else. His main diet was instant mashed potatoes with a can of corn stirred in, or toast with peanut butter and honey. When he went out, it was the small gourmet deli across the street. They had a portabella mushroom, sun dried tomato, provolone, pesto sandwich he lunched on twice a week. There were steps leading down to a rarely frequented section of beach, where John could sit and watch the sea.

Between sips of his beer, he got dressed. Black pants, black turtleneck, and black French beret he had taken a liking to. It saved him the trouble of combing his hair when he had to be around people.

John finished his beer and gargled some mouthwash. There would be the inevitable wine and cheese table, but he now demanded several bottles of Moscato. The whole affair was easier for him to stomach while drinking sweet Italian wine.

The drive North on Pacific Coast Highway passed by a breathtaking beach and house rumored to once have enclosed Sir Elton. John wondered what songs he might have written there, with such a beautiful view.

He arrived at the gallery uncharacteristically early. When the manager saw him coming, he hid the wine key. John's reputation had earned him the nickname among local gallery operators as "the drunk".

John looked around at his work. The prints were very vivid. The prices seemed outrageous. He wondered if he was fooling himself to think art was ever not a commodity. Maybe it had always been an investment, if not for money, for prestige. He chomped on a few pieces of cheese and grabbed a glass.

"You got an opener?"

The manager walked to the table, and made a real show of looking around. He checked the desk drawers, made the motion of patting his pockets, disappeared into a closet for a good ten minutes. He returned to tell John he couldn't find one and would have to send someone to get one, as John was finishing his first glass. He had uncorked a bottle with his pocketknife. The manager muttered something like a prayer under his breath and went into his office to relax.

People started arriving around 7:30. By 8:15 the gallery was filled. By 8:45 John was drunk, despite the meal that had been brought. He was hiding it well. He hadn't said one nasty thing to a single person.

Bruce and his friends decided to say hello. John didn't notice them at first, among so many in typical Newport garb. What was one more plastic surgery disaster in a black dress, or polo shirt with sweater tourniquet? The more he drank, the more he repressed his loathing. The tentative hold he had on the overstretched rubber band of his alcohol induced serenity began to slip as Bruce held a hand in his face smiling.

John looked at the hand, looked at the face, and then recognition dawned on him. He shook Bruce's hand and managed a meager smile.

"Hi John. Glad to see you're one of us now."

John let go of his hand. His smile vanished. The rubber band in his mind broke in two and his body shook as if someone had punched him.

"You phony bastard."

Even at a whisper, his voice was menacing.

"Excuse me?"

John was immediately certain no one had ever talked to Bruce in such a manner. The sardonic smile many people see just before someone shoots them spread across his face.

"You think art is an investment? This is my soul, and you bought it! Like everything else. There's nothing you can't afford, except a soul. And you come here to buy mine. You don't know what art is, because you don't know what life is. Everything's been handed to you, and to you, and to you!

John was standing and pointing at Bruce's friends.

"To all of you!"

He gestured around the room. The manager was wondering what he had done to deserve this humiliation, and came quickly to John's side, grabbing his arm.

"What seems to be the problem?" He said through closed teeth.

John punched him in the jaw, knocking him to the ground.

"You're next!"

He spat at Bruce.

Bruce turned around so fast and ran, his friends were still standing there before they knew what was happening. John picked up the cheese table and smashed it on against the floor. Wielding a table leg he smiled at Bruce's friends.

They ran, and everyone in the gallery flooded out, screaming and yelling, and John began to shout:

"Wave of mutilation, wave of mutilation…"

John noticed a piece by another artist hanging on the wall, brightly colored jungle animal collage style. He knocked it down and urinated on it.

"Where are the dolphins? Where's that goddamned tourist art?!" he screamed.

The manager came to and grabbed John's leg in time to keep him from kicking over a sculpture of a whale in mid leap.

"Have you lost your mind?!" the manager yelled from the ground. "You'll be finished in this town."

"I am finished. Finished being your commodity."

John found his car and drove fast and recklessly down PCH. He saw some people pulled over by the police and slowed his pace. He was in no condition to drive.

In downtown Laguna he parked his car and headed to the hardware store. He walked in smoking and mumbling to himself.

"Sir, you can't smoke in here."

John dropped it where he stood and ground the cigarette into the welcome mat. Composing himself, John looked patiently at the clerk.

The clerk looked back waiting with the patience of one used to dealing with the mentally ill. Perhaps he had been a bus driver for the OCTA before pursuing his current career in hardware.

"Spray paint?"

"Aisle 7."

It was a clean transaction, both men felt satisfied.

John was walking rapidly uphill with a bag under his arm. The church was dark and deserted. On the big wall facing the parking lot, he began to work. A wino with a long gray beard stumbled by, hoarsely croaking some forgotten by the world honky-tonk song. He took no notice of John, inebriated into a whole other world.

Twenty minutes later, his mural complete, John sat on a parking block and surveyed. He removed the last cigarette from a beat up box, crumpled the box and tossed it over his shoulder.

Spray paint was a challenging medium, but the long straw-like attachments made the detail easier to fill in.

A 6-foot Jesus offered a fistful of cash, the other hand clutching the logos of Mercedes Benz, BMW, and Lexus. Little white sheep, with sweaters draped over their shoulders gathered at his feet.

"Okay. Got that off my chest," he said to Jesus.

But he was lying. His outburst at the gallery, his spontaneous graffiti, the alcohol…none of his venting was working. The dam had burst but the water was still standing as if Moses himself was holding it up.

The liquor store was on the way to the sea. He bought a pint of whisky, then stopped at the gas station for a large cup of soda. John mixed the pint into the cup and walked south away from main beach. The waves were breaking hard and the full Moon lit up the water.

Thoughts of lighting his car on fire, throwing away everything in his apartment, and buying a one-way ticket anywhere flashed in his mind like a movie trailer double feature.

John sat down on a dark pile of rocks and regarded the sea. The unmistakable sound of a Zippo lighter caught his ear. He turned around to see a man with a floppy dark green hat and two long braids of hair hanging down each side of his face. The man was sitting crossed legged, silent except for smoking. He reached for his own cigarettes and realized he was out.

"Could I bum one of those?"

The man held out a cigarette.

"You just get off work?"

"No. Sorta. Why?"

"You've got paint all over you."

It was true. He must not have been paying attention and leaned against his mural. At least he wouldn't have left any fingerprints.

"God, what am I doing?"

"I'd say you're getting a good drunk on. By the looks of you, I'd say you've been tagging. Don't worry, I'm not one to turn you in. No love for the police, myself. But I will call you out on that last remark. What the hell are you doing?"

John thought back over the last year and related his story. He talked about Sam, Carrie, and all the people he had met. From shoplifting paint and living in an attic, to having more money than he knew what to do with, he had lost himself somewhere. Himself and two people who were important to him along the way. John unraveled his story to the stranger, whose face was largely invisible in the shadow of his hat. The man's eyes would catch the Moon from time to time as he leaned his head back to exhale smoke.

"There was a time, when I was a kid, when everything was so pure. Black and white clarity with no gray. I knew who the good guys were. I knew who the bad guys were. Lately, I feel like I'm becoming one of them," John said.

The man lit two more cigarettes, handed one to John, and spoke softly.

"So you're trying to sabotage yourself and your success. Only that won't save you."

"What do you mean?"

"Success or not success doesn't make you a good or bad guy. Money or no money doesn't make you a good or bad person. These people who buy your paintings, yes they have money. No, they probably don't give a shit about art. But don't mistake their ignorance for maliciousness. Like it or not, when you really take a look, people are basically good. Their entire focus may be on material accumulation, a repugnant thing to any artist. That doesn't put them in the same category as weapons manufacturers and career politicians.

And you, my friend. You will never be a yuppie, no matter how much money you make. It's not something you can buy your way in to. Being a yuppie is so much more than money. It's almost like being Jewish, as it is a way of preserving continuity with the past through the perpetuation of certain attitudes and traditions.

Even if you wore the pastels and the neck sweaters, drove the overpriced European status-symbol car, you'd still lack that inbred, culturally reinforced feeling of superiority. Give a guy like you money, still not a yuppie. Take a yuppie's money away, still a yuppie. It's attitude. The yuppie will still think they deserve the world on a silver platter.

You're a painter, I'm a poet. We know nobody deserves that, like we know art belongs to all people in all times. So they think they can hang the soul of humanity on their wall? Do you know what happens when a man in his arrogance, purchases the beach, a beautiful painting, or even marries a very attractive woman? Because he has mentally categorized them as possessions, things that one can own, he stops benefiting from the most precious thing they have to offer.

And that's the moment of wonder. The beauty these possess is supposed to make us stop and forget for one minute, all the petty, hectic senselessness of our little lives. And realize there's something more.

John, you paint because you love it. But do you realize the gift you are giving to others? All of us are trapped inside ourselves, locked up with our thoughts and feelings. Language is a poor bridge between us, because I never know if you'll take what I'm saying the right way. But art, art can bring us into communion with one another. It's an attempt to participate in a shared reality. We're the lowest of the low in this world. Laughed at, broke, struggling most of our lives."

And if, the big if…if the crowd takes notice of you in your lifetime, then you risk being consumed by them. Many artists fall from their duty when they try to cater to the mob.

But to hell with them. You create art, because art is needed. It's the soul of humanity. When they spit on you, create. When they shower you with gold, create. The favor of the mob will come and go, but you are the spirit of this time. And that's all that has to make sense to you. You're here now, you interpret what you experience, and you put it out there. Somewhere, someone is looking at your work and thinking she knows just what you mean. And you're not alone, and they are no longer alone. That's the catharsis."

John wiped a tear from his eye.

"You're never quite real, John, until someone sees you for who you really are, and gets you, and doesn't expect anything more from you than to be yourself."

Carrie's face glowed in John's mind.

"I walked away from that person," he said.

"Well start walking back. It's worth a try. It's the most important thing in this world. To connect. That's when we become more. More than these soul cages."

John smiled.

"Thank you. I don't know your name, but thank you."

"I'm Loki. And now I've got to go. Got a plane to catch to Germany in the morning. Have a smoke for the road. And have a book."

Loki handed John a cigarette and a small book of poems.

"And don't ever second guess yourself again."

Loki walked up the stairs and was gone. John sat on the rocks, watching the blue glow of the waves break in the moonlight. The crest would start out at one point and spread to the right and left as it crashed to shore. Little birds with long beaks ran up quickly on toothpick legs to peck tiny creatures from the receding foam.

John resolved to find his way back to Carrie. But first he had to find his car.

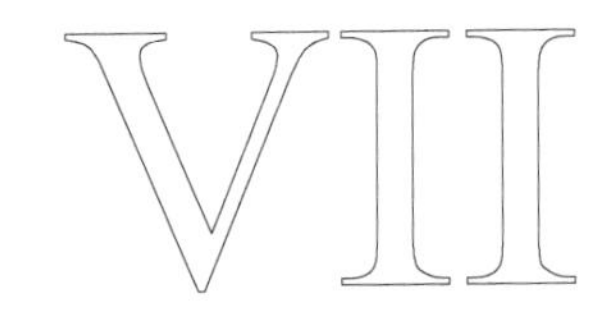

FLASH OF LIGHT

"48, 49, 50."

John collapsed on his back, breathing heavily. He could feel his arms on fire. Starting his morning with push-ups was kind of a pain in the ass. But he hadn't had a cigarette or a drink in a week, and he was starting to feel good about himself.

Mr. Zamensky called to scold John for the fiasco at the Newport gallery and to let him know the spreading rumor of his unpredictable behavior had actually increased the value of his paintings from coast to coast. In part, Mr. Zamensky explained, this was due to an influential New York writer calling John the Charles Bukowski of the art world. John was a little taken aback when Mr. Zamensky asked him if he had really urinated in the gallery.

"I don't remember." Was the best he could come up with.

After much convincing, he went to the gallery and apologized to the manager, telling him he was going to A. A. meetings. It was a lie, but it seemed to smooth things over. John briefly entertained painting a new piece depicting a circle of alcoholics at a meeting with coffee and cigarette shaped monkeys on their backs while a third monkey, in the shape of a Jack Daniel's bottle scampered around the room. It made him laugh, but he felt like an asshole for thinking it.

He finished his morning sit-ups and stood in the kitchen sorting through junk mail. John had a deep-seated urge to find the people that sent him all the garbage and throttle them, or at least make them eat it. A curiously marked envelope lay concealed between the tanning coupons and the liposuction brochure. John fished it out and read: To the Artist John Silverthorne. The return address was an abbreviation: H.R.N.M.

John turned it over, noting the grainy recycled paper making up the envelope. He grabbed his wood carved dragon handle letter opener and tore it apart. The letter inside was printed on the same grainy paper. The contents read:

Dear John,

My name is Ted and I'm part of a grass roots organization called H.R.N.M. or History Repeats No More. I admire your work and would like to ask if we can feature a print of your painting Apocalypse Fruit Basket on our brochures and posters on the danger of global subsistence farming. I think your painting accurately portrays the theme.

Agriculture, as it has been practiced throughout history, creates population explosions that result in over farming, followed by famine and the decline of civilization. Our organization is dedicated to education and prevention of these recurrent trends in human history that threaten the biodiversity of our fragile planet.

We can't offer you much money for the print, but you would be helping a great cause. We are having a gathering at our house in Mission Viejo this Saturday night. You should come by and meet some of the most visionary thinkers in Orange County.
Sincerely,
Ted Moobakfle

John found the idea appealing in some penitent corner of his self-concept. He also liked the idea of contributing his art without any trace of financial transaction. John felt a need to give without taking, though he cared fuck-all what civilization did to itself. He had to keep going with the repair and reinvention of himself. The only cause he had fought for was his own survival. That issue seemed to have passed.

John examined the contents of his apartment again. It was just stuff, neither inherently good nor bad. Loki's book of poetry was lying on top of the turntable. He flipped it open to a poem.

Sing a Golden Song
Die radiantly, singing a golden song
Painting the wind with the melody
Of your Soultones true and strong
And when the archon bars the way
Of your journey to the luminous shore
Sing out: "I see you have not known me,
Thinking me the clothes I wore!"

All his life, the guillotine of his judgment passed quickly over everyone he met. Orange County had only sharpened the blade. Deep down, he was acknowledging the anger that had been slowly killing him. He wasn't about to run out and join the yacht club, but he wanted to try giving people a chance on an individual basis.

John inhaled deeply. His lungs were going to need time to heal. He didn't want to think about his liver. A sigh of determination helped clear his mind.

Something told him there had been a knocking sound on his door for probably 5 minutes. John opened the door to see a priest standing there with a bucketful of cleaning supplies. He blinked to make sure it wasn't a hallucination.

"Can I help you?"

The man had gray thin hair combed to one side, offset by youthful blue eyes. A gentle smile raised rosy cheeks. He looked like a mirthful grandfather.

"Son, I'm here to help *you.*"

"Um. I'm not really inclined to religion, father."

"I'm here to keep you out of jail, not to convert you."

John felt his stomach fall down an elevator shaft.

"How do you propose to help me, father?"

"I'd like you to come down to the church and clean up the wall. I've got you a bucket of graffiti removing supplies. When you finish that, it would be nice if you could touch up some of the fading parts of our religious paintings inside the church. I spoke with your agent, Mr. Zamensky, and he thought it was a fair trade for avoiding jail. He told me you're trying to clean up your life. I believe in second chances. What do you say?"

John smiled and took the bucket from the priest.

"Thank you."

Across town, sawdust, buckets of paint, and the din of hammering and drilling surrounded Carrie. The brewing tanks had been installed. The walk-in refrigerators and freezers, and most of the kitchen were done. They had entered into the last phase of construction, with the sanding and shaping of the bar and painting the interior. The wiring was done, the lights hung. It was mostly finishing touches, which would take a good month. Then Carrie would have to hire the staff and prepare the press for the opening.

Carrie had never been busier in her life, but she felt great. She continued sanding away on the bar. At the other end, her Dad was riveting smooth sheets of copper that gave the counter an iridescent quality. It was also easy to clean.

She stopped sanding and felt the wood. It was considerably smooth to the touch. Carrie decided the long counter was finally done being sanded. Once her dad put the rest of the copper sheeting down, it would be finished.

Wiping sweat from her forehead, Carrie removed her safety glasses. They had been keeping the doors shut to keep the construction sounds from bothering the neighboring businesses. The weather was warming up, and she didn't see the harm in opening a window.

The ocean's salty breeze kissed her nose. She got the spontaneous urge to take a walk. She took off her smock and put her hand on her father's shoulder.

"Dad, I'm going to take a little stroll. I'll be back in a few minutes."

"Can you get me some more rivets?"

"Sure."

He handed her an empty box.

"Just take this to the hardware store, and they'll give you the same size."

"Okay, Dad."

Carrie stepped out onto the sidewalk, squinting at the brightness of the day. She meandered toward the hardware store. Pedestrian traffic was getting thick, a sure sign of the coming tourist season.

The hardware store was frigid. Their air conditioner must have been set too low and left on over night. Carrie felt like she had entered the polar bear section of the zoo. She thought she could almost see her breath. Then her heart sank.

Standing in front of her, reflecting her own wounded animal expression was John. He was holding a can of graffiti remover.

A million thoughts went through her head in just a few seconds. Was it really him? We were bound to run into each other eventually, right? Should I say hi? Is he mad at me? Have I gained weight? Is he seeing someone new? He looks thinner, has he lost weight? Is he going to say hi or just stand there looking stupid? Should I turn around and-?

"Hi, Carrie."

This wasn't how John wanted to see her again-in a hardware store, by accident. He felt a wave of anxiety as her eyes went cold and calm. Carried turned around and walked to the cash register.

John stood in line behind her wanting to say anything but the wrong thing.

"How have you been, Carrie?"

Carrie kept her back turned and didn't respond. Then she turned around quickly to face him.

"How have I been? That's not what I'm waiting to hear, John."

John felt like an already sinking ship getting hit by a tidal wave.

"Um. How's the business?"

Carrie paid for the rivets.

"No, that's not it either."

She had an angry smile.

"9 months, John. 9 months! No word?"

He was in that peculiar state of human affairs where he'd been kicking himself, and now someone else adds their kicking feet to the wound.

"What do you want me to say?"

He followed her out onto the sidewalk. The hardware store cashier just shook his head.

"How about sorry? How about you miss me? How about you really blew it?"

She was yelling. John put his head down for a moment, then slowly looked up directly into her eyes.

"I've missed you terribly. I am more sorry then I've ever been. And I know I blew it, and you were the best thing in my life."

Carrie smiled sardonically.

"Thanks, John. See you around."

She walked briskly away with John trailing after.

"Wait, Carrie!"

"No! I'm done waiting."

"I said I was sorry."

She stopped.

"Good. Now stay the hell away from me."

She started walking again.

"Carrie, give me another chance!"

"What am I supposed to do, John? Let you hurt me again? Trust you and have you walk away from me again?"

Carrie stopped and as nicely as she could manage, folded her hands and politely smiled.

"I hope you find happiness. I'm glad you have become so successful with your art. I have my own life to think about, on my own. Okay? Please, I'm really busy."

John was about to plead and beg, but he noticed a man in the doorway behind Carrie. It was her dad.

"Did you get the rivets, Carrie?"

"Yes. Yes I did. Dad, you remember my friend John, don't you?"

Carrie's dad looked from John to Carrie and knew he had just stepped into a hornet's nest. Her mom used the same kind of argumentative ploy.

"Yes, I remember. Hi, John."

"Hi."

"John was just leaving. Nice seeing you, John. Come by and try the food, when we open."

She smiled cordially.

It was the first time he had seen her be fake, but in fairness, he blamed himself for driving her to it.

"I'll do that" he said.

It felt bitter on his tongue, and when he swallowed he felt ravenously empty. He went back to the church, feeling like a balloon almost out of helium, stumbling numbly about the city.

Carrie wished hard that the aching would stop. She wanted to feel good about telling him off, wanted to humiliate him, to smack him hard across the face. But deep down she wondered if he didn't feel as alone and hurt as she did.

She was in the bathroom, getting some sawdust out of her eyes that had blown in right about the time John had left.

Her dad knew better than to try to offer advice when a woman was hurting. His policy was to give them space. Twenty-five years of marriage seemed to give his theory credibility.

He continued working steadily on finishing the counter. A man should be reliable, consistent, not given to unpredictable behavior, he mused. That's how you keep a woman happy. Make them feel insecure, uncertain, and rue the day.

The private thoughts of Carrie's dad may have given John some needed guidance in a dark hour. But he was across town, smelling of paint thinner and other solvents, maybe a little woozy from the fumes. He finally finished scrubbing away the last of his mural. John went in to the rectory and found the father reading. The old man looked up kindly.

"It's all done. It's gone."

"Splendid."

He rose and put his hand on John's shoulder.

"Let me walk you around the church and you tell me what materials we need to touch up the holy paintings. We will buy the paint, don't you worry, brushes, whatever you need."

"Okay."

"We really appreciate such a talented artist as yourself donating your time like this."

John couldn't tell if he was messing with him, but he seemed sincere.

"No problem."

They stopped in front of a small scene of the nativity. The blue was flaking off Mary's robes and the flesh tones of all the figures were fading.

"I got the paint for this at home, no problem."

"We can reimburse you."

"No, Father, I would like it if you let me donate the paint as well as my time. I'm kind of new at thinking of others. I would like it if you let me."

"Thank you, son."

The next scene was Jesus praying in the garden of Gethsemane. John could tell the original creator had used a projector and traced the details carefully from a classic painting. It was in the humanist style, but he couldn't put a name to it. The details were fading and Jesus' nose was off-color. The people who filled the pews probably never got close enough to notice these things, which told John the priest was fond of spending time in front of them.

They came to the last scene that needed revamping. John was taken aback. It was Mary Magdalene at the tomb of Jesus. A halo adorned her head and above the tomb was a bright glowing light like a small sun. Two Roman soldiers were shielding their eyes, but Mary seemed to regard the brilliance with a smile.

The priest could see John was thinking hard.

"John, what is it?"

John came out of his reverie a little hazily, half entranced, speaking like a sleepwalker.

"This piece…is like a drawing I just did. See these guards are turning away, but Mary…Mary is looking right at the light, because for the first time in her life she feels real. Like she's living in reality. She sees herself in the light, and the light has brought her into the kingdom of god…the kingdom of the real…beyond the false light of the world, which light might as well be darkness…"

He trailed off.

"Son where did you study this painting?"

The priest had a strange look on his face.

"I didn't, but love is like that. I guess in this piece it's the love of god or whatever, sorry Father, like I said I'm not religious. And in my drawing it's…the light of love."

"Sounds like the same thing."

"Father, I've got to go, I'm…inspired. But I'll be back to fix up the paintings. Thanks."

He rushed out the door.

"Ah, youth." The priest looked at the picture he had painted so long ago and smiled.

John raced home and returned to a canvas he had drawn the outline for at 4 a.m. Woken by a vivid dream, he had made the sketch by candlelight. There was a beautiful sketch of Carrie's face surrounded by light shooting out from behind her head. A room was less and less visible moving away from the light source.

John used a chiaroscuro technique laying in the darks and lights, and then bathed the dim sections in a blue gray, revealing a bookcase, a spilled glass of water, and vines with small flowers. He did the pulsing halo in vivid yellows and gold. The flesh tones and red of the lips added a super realistic quality to the dreamy piece. He would call it 'Flash of Light'.

Setting up four more blank canvases, he circled around and around, stopping and sketching in details. Using the same concept, John sketched her next to a lattice overlooking a garden, reaching for a volume at the bookcase, lying asleep head cradled in arm, and at the end of a very long hallway. Preliminary sketches finished, he worked diligently in a trance, painting and detailing.

The phone rang a few times, but John was too absorbed to hear it. Day became night and the rapid temperature drop peculiar to beach cities roused him to close the window. The muse had him by the heartstrings, and he wouldn't see his bed before dawn.

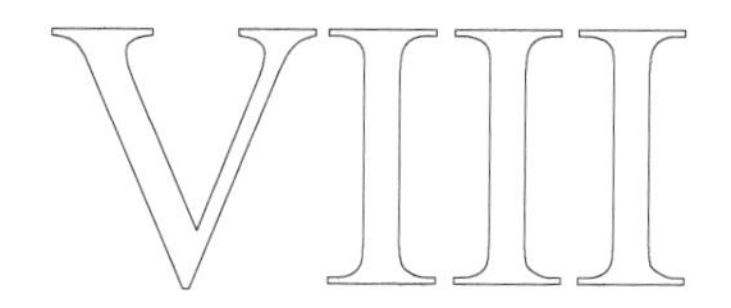

Green House

John pulled his car into the grocery store parking lot. He didn't know what to expect from the H.R.N.M crowd. He thought it would be nice to bring a bottle of wine to the party.

Inside the store he quickly found the wine aisle. He walked up and down the cool aisles. A man in a Hawaiian shirt and an apron came over to where John was standing perplexed.

"Can I help you, sir?"

John scratched his head and looked around the racks.

"Um. Do you have any Moscato?"

"Moscato? Never heard of it."

John sighed.

"Then I guess not."

He perused the Merlots, settling on a California brand a couple of years old. It was a safe gift, and who knew if these people even drank wine? It was better than arriving empty-handed.

There were no fast checkout lanes, reminding John how he loathed shopping. Maybe he'd just been squandering his grocery time his whole life, by buying only a few items. It seemed everyone else knew better filling their carts to capacity like dutiful Mormons stocking up for the end of the world. Maybe a full cupboard was what allowed people to sleep at night.

John pulled a pen from his pocket, grabbed a magazine mailer out of the nearest rag, and sketched a gaunt man standing in front of an open and barren cupboard. He drew huge bags under the man's eyes and added candles burnt low, wax spilling over. Underneath he wrote "The insomniac".

"I can help you over here, Sir."

John came out of his trance and moved to a different register. He paid and walked out of the store. Parking lots in Laguna Hills were especially treacherous due to the geriatric drivers.

As he drove out of the parking lot, John noticed the Moon was out. The Sun had not yet set. It reminded him of alchemical drawings from the renaissance period. He thought of the Moon card in the tarot deck and the howling animals and sea monsters it portrayed. What made the coyote howl? Was it solitude or that one big eye staring down?

The 'Green House' was situated up on a hill and lived up to its name in natural fecundity. She had been busy. The front yard was right out of National Geographic with bush, leaves, flowers and trees haphazardly encroaching everything. The occupants must have periodically hacked a path to the front door with a machete. John wondered if he should come back later, inoculated.

John turned off his car and watched a few tie died long hairs enter the domicile.

"Stop being judgmental, stop being judgmental."

He repeated it like a mantra. Taking a deep breath, John walked up the path, noting the green paint was one of his favorite shades. The door opened before he could knock.

"What's in the bag?"

An older man in his 60's with a shaved head and bristly whiskers eyed John suspiciously.

"Wine."

The old man reached out.

"Let's see."

John handed him the paper bag.

"Merlot? I guess this will do. Loaded with sulfites, though. Next time bring organic."

He shoved the bottle back into John's hands and disappeared inside the house. The door stood agape.

"This is probably my last chance to get the hell out of here."

John entered the house and shut the door behind him. The music was loud, sounded vaguely like Neil Young, and made all the conversations louder. John thought Neil Young sounded like a Muppet with syphilis.

There was a living room to the left, and behind the stairs to the right another one. Facing him, leaning at an odd angle, was a large mirror. Above the mirror someone had fingerpainted in green Do n 't Ge t St u ck.

"It means don't get stuck in your ego trip."

A young man with long blonde dreadlocks and a friendly demeanor was smiling at John.

"I'm Jahsin."

"John. You live here?"

"No, just came by for the gathering."

The old man reappeared in the hall. He had a bottle of beer in each hand and one shoved in his front pocket.

"We call him Grandpa. He's a writer, drinks like a fish, and his granddaughter comes over every now and then. Watch out for his conspiracy theories. Oh, shit. Here he goes."

Grandpa was standing at the door hugging a young woman with a backpack.

"That's his granddaughter."

Grandpa took her bag.

"You didn't bring any toothpaste this time, I hope?"

"No Grandpa."

He rifled through the bag and pulled out a pair of shoes. He reached his hand inside of one and then the other. His eyes widened with dismay, as he removed a small traveler's size toothpaste from one of the shoes.

The girl blushed.

"How many times have I told you about the danger of fluoride? It's a toxin. Hitler wanted it added to drinking water to help control people. He knew it makes you docile and weakens your immune system. THEY want you to use it. Come on."

Grandpa pulled her by the arm. Jahsin was grinning. He motioned for John to follow.

In the downstairs bathroom, the old man finished applying a large squirt of liquid anti-bacterial soap to the girl's toothbrush.

"Now brush for ten minutes."

She brushed while grandpa looked at his watch.

"How embarrassing. Have you met, Ted?"

"No, but he's the one who invited me."

"Let me introduce you."

Jahsin lead John up the stairs. They passed a very large room to the right where a number of people were talking and drinking. He saw a beautiful girl with short red hair kissing a scruffy man on a couch, and he felt the pangs of missing Carrie.

On the opposite side 2nd room to the left, wild laughter echoed from behind the door. Jahsin flung the door open.

"What's going on?!"

"Hey, Jahsin. Come in, sit down."

Ted had the kind of hair that left to its own would become a crazy afro. He looked vaguely Columbian and had a sinister grin on his face. John wasn't sure what to make of it.

"Canadian t.v. is the best. They're allowed to say motherfucker," he chuckled. "I downloaded the entire season of Mobile Home Lads."

He shut down his computer and took a few swallows of wine. John noticed it was Pinot Grigio. There was an empty bottle of it next to the computer monitor.

"Hi. I'm Ted Moobakfle."

He shook John's hand.

"John Silverthorne."

"I'm glad you came. I'm also glad you don't shake hands like a nancy. I hate all that hand jive bullshit. Have you seen the house?"

"Part of it."

"Let me show you the rest."

As they went into the hallway a man emerged from the master bedroom at the end of the hall. He was dressed in a plaid kilt and an African shirt. His long curly hair reminded John of Tiny Tim.

"Ted, do you know anything about why the lamp downstairs isn't working?"

"No idea."

Ted tried to continue walking.

"It was working yesterday, now it isn't."

"Pat, I don't know."

He tried to take another step.

"That's strange that it would just randomly stop functioning. You don't have any idea?"

Ted glared at the man.

"It was working yesterday, and now mysteriously it doesn't work."

Ted took a deep breath, then pointed his finger at Pat.

"Shut up you skirt wearing mic. I don't know anything about the goddamn lamp. I don't like repeating myself."

Pat stopped curling his hair around his finger for a moment.

"O.K., I'll ask Grandpa."

"Grandpa's been drinking. You might not want to antagonize him right now."

Pat practically skipped downstairs to find Grandpa.

"Sorry about that, John. Total nancy. He thinks he's Irish. It was actually the English who came up with the kilt. It's a shorter version of the Tartan. The English invaded and screwed all the Irish women. Nancy like that, he's got to be British. Let me show you the backyard, where we grow the veggies."

Once again John wondered what to make of Ted's sinister grin. Jahsin followed behind. They pushed passed a crowd of people into the backyard.

"We call this the little Green House. Cute, huh?"

In the backyard stood a structure about 8 foot high by 12 feet wide by 12 feet long. Ted pulled back a flap of plastic tarp and they entered.

"Welcome to the world of Hydroponics!"

Covering the shelves of various levels were all sorts of plants growing strictly in water. There were tomatoes, beans, lettuces, soybeans, and what looked like marijuana. John had never seen horticulture of this sort.

"This is our solution for the inevitable agricultural collapse brought on by traditional agriculture. You ever hear of the Mayan calendar?"

John looked at Ted and thought of a carving or mosaic shaped like a sun or a pizza he had seen once. He shook his head.

"You talk to some of these hippies in here, and they'll try to tell you the Mayan people just disappeared one day. Vanished. Also, that their calendar abruptly ends in December of 2012, and that there's going to be some kind of spiritual event or cataclysm. Only, it's a bunch of crap. The Mayan didn't vibrate into some higher spiritual realm. They're still with us today, in Mexico and all over Orange County. Don't let these people run off at the mouth to you about it. Archaeologists have been able to demonstrate by studying the known rate of accumulation of hydrogen molecules upon obsidian blades, at different levels of occupation, and by taking core samples from trees, the Mayan centers declined over a 500-year period. Maybe that's not exciting enough for the average bong-rip trooper, but that's what the evidence supports."

"You see what happened was, the way they irrigated and farmed the land, it raised the saline level in the soil. When it reached the root level, the crops had massive failures. They had to abandon their city centers and the jungle gradually reclaimed them. This is a classic scenario that happens over and over throughout the world."

"California farms are facing the same crises right at this moment. Saline levels have been rising, and agricultural collapse is imminent. Which is why we are trying to educate people and come up with a way to produce agriculture without soil."

"Now in classic subsistence farming, where people live off their crops but don't usually work to produce surplus, it can take up to 10 acres of land to feed one person. This method of growing is a lot of effort for a low yield, not to mention all the water used. Our challenge has been to come up with a blend of the most nutritious foods, that form complete carbohydrates, provide full servings of protein, and are loaded with amino acids, while utilizing the smallest amount of space and the least water. If we don't succeed, the civilization cycle is doomed to repeat over and over. Of course we're amateurs and hacks, but Einstein said imagination is more important than intelligence. We may not be Harvard scientists, but we are creative people who can think outside the box."

"That's why I thought your painting was an appropriate symbol for our organization. A basket of fruit and yet the mood of impending doom. I think it sums up the cycle of histories failed methods."

John was feeling a little overwhelmed by this barrage of information. He viewed the hippy movement as something derailed by drugs, and these people were growing pot. As far as John could tell, changing the world, at least economically or socially required vast sums of money and power. H.R.N.M. seemed like one more pipe dream. Still, Ted did seem sincere, and it wasn't like it would hurt John in any way.

"Alright. You can use the print on your brochures. But please, for the sake of my agent, who doesn't like the idea of giving anything away for free, don't make any normal size posters."

Ted grinned his sinister grin.

"No problem."

The flap opened and a man made a hand gesture at Ted and stuck out his tongue. Ted did it back to the guy.

"Excuse me, I have to attend to something for a moment. Feel free to mingle. And don't let that nancy interrogate you."

John was feeling ancy. He hadn't been around drinking and smoking since he gave them up. John wasn't sure what to do with himself.

About a dozen people had gathered in the living room by the front door. They were wearing nametags and someone was reciting some kind of rules.

"The final rule is: if it's your first night at Poetry Club, you have to read."

Someone handed him a nametag and a black marker.

"Make up a name and stick it to yourself." They whispered. "Also, write your made up name on the peeled off part and throw that in the hat. Names are drawn randomly, and you can do a poem, a song, or whatever."

John looked at the man's nametag. It said, "Dynamite the Capital". He thought for a minute and wrote "Heronymous Bosch".

A girl with a nametag that said "Christ!" drew the names. The people clapped after each person read or sang a song, which seemed strange at first, but John decided it gave everyone an added confidence. He was no poet, but he figured what the hell.

"Heronymous Bosch." Christ! said.

John smoothed out the paper he had been scribbling on.

Most of the people were watching him, others were scribbling, he heard the sound of a guitar being tuned coming from upstairs. Ted stood up, looked toward the master bedroom and made a squealing monster noise.

"Hey Fucko, rule three, stop making noise up there and have some respect."

The door slammed.

"Please continue."

John cleared his throat, and stood up.

"I'm not a poet, but I wrote down something I've been thinking about. I apologize if it sucks."

"When no one could see me,
You saw.
When no one could hear me,
You heard.
When no one could touch me,
You taught me to feel again.
If you don't forgive me for
Acting the fool,
I will be invisible,
Soundless,
And numb once more.
I blew it.
But you make me want to try again."

"That's it."

The people clapped and John sat down. The man known as Pat came downstairs with his guitar, just as Christ! read his nametag.

"I'd like to play a song by my favorite Irish band. This song is about oppression, and I just think the passion of the singer is so inspiring…"

Ted was rolling his eyes. Jahsin was now next to John. He leaned into John's ear.

"He always gives the same speeches. It's like a series of monologues he has memorized."

"Is that good?" John asked.

"It seems very fake and contrived to Ted and I."

Pat started playing the song and Ted scowled at the ceiling, like he was telling God he would pay one day.

"They don't like each other?"

"You have no idea," Jahsin said. "This house full of creative people, hates each other."

"Wow. That sucks. Why?"

"It's like everyone is trying to be the alpha male, trying to dominate the others. And then the girls are a big issue. It's like a competition. Let's go out back and talk, I've heard this song a million times."

They went to the backyard.

"I thought you guys were trying to save the world?"

John tried to ask the question without it being an accusation.

"When we started the group, we were really into eco-village ideas and this house seemed like a place where Ted could experiment by living with other artists. I don't know if I want to live on an eco-village now."

John fiddled with his sleeve.

"What's an eco-village?"

"It's a place where people live together and grow their own food. You try to make a self-sustaining environment, meaning everything necessary for life is produced there."

"Kind of like the Amish?"

"Uh. Yeah, I guess. But it's not a religion or a cult. There are a bunch of them all over the world."

"Have you ever been to any?"

"One near San Diego."

"What did you think?"

A possum scurried across the top of the fence.

"The place I went to had been there for 10 years. They had only a few structures and the green house was pretty small.

It seemed like they were a bunch of squatters. Nothing was really going on."

"Sounds like you were pretty disappointed."

"Yeah. I was. I met this lady named Eve. That made it worth the trip."

"What was she like?"

"Everyday I was there she was giving massages. She was around 50 years old with a short Zen Buddhist haircut. The egos were a big problem there, too. Eve told us there was a lot of little power struggles, and nothing got done at any certain time. All the chores rotated, but people were very lackadaisical about when they did them. She liked order, so it was challenging for her. Eve also told us about the spiritual masters she had studied under, and how scandalous they all were."

"Scandalous?"

"Turns out her Zen master was sleeping with his students. She burned her robes and gave back the lineage papers to him. That's probably the biggest insult you could give to a teacher. Eve said he was fuming. I couldn't believe all the famous masters that she knew who were sleeping with their students. Scandalous."

John thought about it for a minute.

"So do you feel disillusioned from talking to her?"

"I don't know what to think right now. I'm just trying to focus on myself."

"I hear you."

A match flared up as a younger Mexican man stepped from the shadows. He was smoking a joint.

"Hi, H.T." Said Jahsin.

H.T. had shoulder length black hair and a faint mustache. His brown eyes were like deep wells of thought. He smiled at Jahsin and passed the joint.

"Jahsin, there was a time my dream was to go to Mexico and join the Zapatistas in their resistance against the Mexican government. Now I've found taking care of my little brother and my Mom is more important to me. I'm tired of all political rhetoric, anarchist rhetoric, and activist rhetoric."

"I think the thing to do is take care of your family first. That's the number one thing. Look what happened after the industrial revolution. People who once lived with their families and extended families including their grandparents, moved away to work in some capitalists factory. If we want to see all that change, first we take care of the immediate family, Mother, father and siblings. Then we take care of the extended family, grandma and grandpa. Then the extended family becomes a group of extended families in your neighborhood called the band. Then the neighborhoods of extended families become a cluster, which we call community and the tribe. Everyone knows everyone else. Everyone talks to each other. We work together for our mutual benefit. Then the communities become clusters of communities and become the nation. A confederacy of tribes working together, governed from the bottom up. Not the top down way of centralized government. The leadership is in the family. And we are all one family."

H.T. smiled as he took the last hit of the joint. He walked around the side of the house to relieve his bladder in the bushes.

Ted came outside, looking surly. He put his hand on Jahsin's shoulder.

"Turkey's of Satan moves to the final phase."

John gave them both a puzzled look. Ted grinned.

"We'd tell you, but it's safer for you if you don't know."

After the poetry reading, all hell broke loose. Grandpa kept dancing lewdly and falling over. Ted threw a bottle against the wall, sending glass in all directions. Pat had ducked just in time to avoid catching it with his face. John decided it was time to leave.

As he got in his car and turned on the stereo, he saw flames shooting up the side of the house.

"What the hell?"

He craned his head back to see everyone pouring out of the house onto the street. Rather than stick around he hit the accelerator. Turning the corner he thought he heard that squealing monster noise Ted had made, echoing through the neighborhood, followed by a sinister laugh.

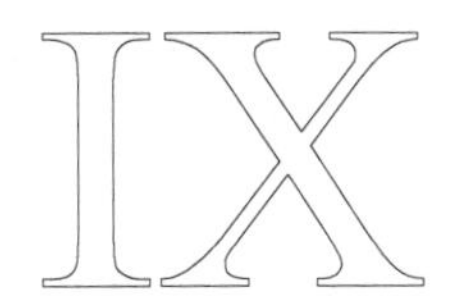

INTRODUCTION

At 5 A.M. there were few people on the beach. One or two joggers, or early morning dog walkers, but John hadn't seen anyone since he climbed over some large rocks. He was walking south, and every time he reached a barrier he climbed over it.

The old nagging voices were taking shots at John. He had cleaned up, and the long neglected raw nerves had a message for him. He was alone in a lonely hour.

A little gravel slid under his feet. John regained his balance. He was high up on a cliff, trying to get to the other side. If he fell, it was a good 20 feet or more onto some jagged rocks. Vertigo seized him for a moment. He squatted down and closed his eyes.

Taking a deep breath, he willed the dizziness away and stood up. There was no way down the other side without death or serious injury. He didn't want to turn back.

As the tide rushed in and out, he saw an opportunity to hang from his hands and drop onto some rocks. If he timed it right he could get to the beach without getting slammed against the rocks by the waves. He waited for the right moment.

Dangling over the rushing water, he heard the sucking sound get louder and let go. One boot landed on the rock, one came down in 4 inches of water. He quickly jumped from rock to rock, and then ran along the cave wall, emerging on the sand just ahead of an inrushing wave.

John turned around and regarded the coast he had left behind. He sat down as a wave of emotional anguish mixed with hunger washed over him. If only he could walk away from his past the way he could walk away from Main Beach. It was no good. Some things had to be faced or they would forever chew away at a man, like a tapeworm coiled around his soul.

John examined his thoughts like taking apart a spider web strand by strand. He found there were four distinct personalities within him: the artist, who created for the love of expression, in love with Nature and her mysteries; the philosopher who devoured books and sought the highest realms of thought and emotion; the cynic, who looked with suspicion upon people and institutions, who had buried too much for one so young and had a deep well of secret pain; and the unpredictable child who acted out in acts of vandalism, theft, or promiscuity.

A high school guidance councilor had mentioned to a 16 year old John that he may suffer from disassociative behavior.

"What the hell is that?" John had asked.

"John, you don't have to tell me what kind of abuse you have been through, but when children are physically and/or sexually abused, they sometimes develop other personalities to cope with the abuse. This allows them to detach from what is happening and escape into a fantasy life. It's similar to having imaginary friends, only these ones are inside of you. You create a personality or personalities that feel no pain, or are immune to loneliness."

"I've noticed you come to school dressed as a totally different type of person almost every day. How come you don't pick a group and stick with it?"

John had winced.

"I think the cliques here are stupid. I wear different clothes to mock the whole idea."

"Don't you want to fit in?"

"I don't care. I don't think these other kids could really understand me."

"Why do you feel that way, John?"

"Because they haven't had the experiences I've had. They haven't traveled, they haven't been in the places I've been."

This was the first time John had verbalized his feelings, and he didn't like doing it with this adult he didn't trust.

"John, has it occurred to you that the other students here have probably had experiences you haven't had?"

"Yeah, right. They've probably lived in this little town their whole lives. They'll graduate from this high school, go to the college, and get married and live here until they die. I don't have anything in common with them. In one year I've lived and done more than they will ever do."

This sixteen-year-old kid was making the councilor uncomfortable.

"That's not really fair, John. You should give them a chance, you could probably learn things from them."

John had grown up with his Italian Grandfather and Italian Mother. He had been practicing the art of argument almost from his first words. He could sense weakness like a shark could smell blood. John felt the councilor's confidence in reaching him weaken. He moved in for the kill.

"Did you grow up here?"

The councilor swallowed hard.

"Yes."

"You ever lived anywhere else?"

"No."

"I'm done talking to you."

John walked out of the man's office and a few months later he had left the state for another of the five high schools he would attend. Trying to face himself in the present, John wondered if there was something to what the man had said. He had flipped through a psychology book once and read the challenge of disassociative tendencies was to integrate the personalities into one whole person.

"How do I do this?"

John spoke to the sea.

"I don't want to integrate, I want to get rid of them. I don't want to be cynical. I don't want to act unpredictably."

The sea offered her deep blue embrace, and her patient listening skills. John didn't have to wonder why he preferred Nature to people. Nature knew how to listen. He learned stillness and grace from Nature.

John picked up a piece of bamboo that lay entwined with seaweed. He freed it from the salty plant and drew a life-size silhouette of a human figure. With horizontal lines he divided it into four sections. In the head he wrote the letter A for Artist. On the heart area he inscribed the Greek letter phi for Philosopher. He made a C over the stomach to represent the Cynic in him. Finally he made a CH in the pelvic region for the Child.

"Well?"

An enormous swell came up and crashed over John and his drawing. He was soaked and laughing at himself. The drawing was wiped out completely. John stood up chuckling.

"Is that a baptism or are you saying my theory doesn't hold water?"

He laughed his way up the beach access stairs and onto the street. A bus went by hurling cold air and debris at him. John closed his eyes tight until it passed.

A half hour later he was back in his apartment in dry clothing. Message from Mr. Z. about upcoming shows. Message from priest about painting. Message from Sam about dinner, please call cell phone.

John excitedly copied down the number and picked up the phone. It rang three times.

"Hello?"

"Sam?"

"John, is that you, you bastard?" Sam's voice was mirthful.

"What are you doing in town?"

"Visiting family. I thought I'd offer you a chance to bury the hatchet."

"Well, I accept."

"Great. What do you say about dinner tonight?"

"Sure."

"You in the same place?"

"Yeah."

"I'll come by around 6."

"Sam, it's good to hear from you. I'll see you tonight."

John hung up. He went to his canvases leaning against the wall. Mr. Z. wanted the "Flash of Light" series for the next show. John had already had the prints made, and looking at the original with Carrie's pretty face, he felt he couldn't ever sell the original. There was only one person he wanted to give it to.

"What the hell? Why not?"

John lay the painting down on thick brown construction paper and wrapped it in several layers. He taped it up and put it by the door. Taking a deep breath he sat down. If there was ever a time to write a letter, this was it.

Dear Carrie,

I hope you will accept this painting whatever you decide. It's called "Flash of Light" because you light up the world wherever you go.

Love,
John

John put the letter in an envelope and taped it to the brown paper covering the painting. He put on his French beret and marched down the street. Dark clouds had rolled in off the sea and it looked like rain. Picking up the pace he almost tripped on a crack in the sidewalk, but regained his balance.

At Carrie's front door on Daisy Lane he knocked three times.

"Oh, idiot."

John's watch read 8:30 A.M. He started to set the painting down when the door opened a crack, startling him. Composing himself he made a half-assed smile. Blonde curly hair and narrow eyes blinked a few times.

"What do you want?"

"Is Carrie here?"

"Are you going to be nice if I get her?"

John looked at his feet.

"I'm not here to fight. I want to apologize."

Jane examined him. He seemed sober. It was probably a good thing he had shaved.

"Okay. I'll see if I can wake her. But if you pull anymore shit, I'll kill you myself."

She shut the door leaving him outside. A few uncomfortable minutes went by and it was all John could do to not take off. Finally he heard the handle turning.

"She doesn't want to talk to you."

Jane's look was hard to read. John thought she was willing to give him a chance but still felt suspicion. Carrie was another story.

"Will you give her this?"

John held up the wrapped up painting with attached letter. Jane pulled it inside and looked at John sympathetically.

"I'll make sure she gets it. See you later, John."

She shut the door and locked it. John sighed and walked home feeling dejected while holding onto the smallest grain of hope. It began to rain.

By the time he got home he was soaked. It was really pouring and thunder shook the windows. John put a fresh canvas on an easel and stripped off his clothes. He lit candles and instead of using his complex stereo, he hit play on his old cassette player.

"...Whores at the door..." It sang.

John let the tears come as he painted a naked man, hugging his knees in the corner of blue walls. Shackles with dangling broken chains hung from the man's wrists and John masterfully rendered a moist appearance to the flesh under his eyes.

"...We're Chai-ained..."

In the crosshatched shadowing of black paint he hid a heart with initials. The lighting and blurred quality recalled the work of Francis Bacon. This was painting as exorcism.

It occurred to John that there were some good things in the parts of himself he didn't like. If it wasn't for his unpredictable side, he might not have the guts to go to Carrie's door and try to make amends. Without the cynic, he wouldn't have that well of pain that was the flip side of joy. How could he portray nature in only one aspect? Without his pain, he'd be painting those god-awful smiling dolphins.

Exhausted from a busy morning he lay down on the floor and lost consciousness.

The phone was ringing in John's dream. He was standing on the sea and not sinking, painting a whale wearing a tuxedo that was so kind as to pose on top of the water for him. John thought to himself how illogical a phone ringing in the middle of the ocean was, though the whale in the tux made perfect sense to his dreaming self.

The answering machine kicked on and he began to sink.

"I'm awake. I'm awake."

John sat up and looked at the machine with dismay. He could live in a world without answering machines and alarm clocks and not shed a single tear.

"John, are you there? John pick up."

It was Sam. John got up on his feet and picked up the handset.

"Yeah, I'm here."

"You sleeping?"

"Off and on. I've been painting and napping all day."

"I was thinking you could meet me instead of me coming by. I've got to bail right after dinner."

"Okay. Where at?"

"Let's hit the Mexican joint."

"See you there."

John drove through the rain past the street that led to Carrie's house and up Pacific Coast Highway to a parking spot on the hill. He could see the ocean as he crossed the street to the restaurant.

The gray choppy water reminded him of being in preschool and discovering all the finger paints mixed together made a dull gray color. It seemed so mysterious when he was a kid. How could blue and red and green disappear into that murk? And he had wondered if there was a way to get them back out. He had tried, that curious kid. Even then he wasn't apt to listen to anyone telling him he was being foolish. Foolishness seemed like the way to go. The way of the Fool was the way into mystery.

Sam was waiting just inside the door. He gave John a big hug.

"John it's good to see you."

"Sam I'm really sorry about-"

"Don't mention it. It's in the past. We don't have to live there or even visit."

The host sat them in a booth and brought water.

"What are you drinking these days, John? You want a Guinness?"

"Actually, I don't drink anymore."

Sam looked at him seriously. "Really? What brought that on?"

John couldn't help laughing a little. "Your friend Bruce."

"Bruce?"

"Yeah. I was drunk and I was going to beat the shit out of him, but he ran away. So I tagged a church and barely avoided jail. You won't believe it, I've been helping touch up the old paintings inside that church on the hill."

"I didn't think anything would get you to set foot in there."

"Beats the hell out of a felony. Point is, I realized I was getting out of control, and it was time for a change."

"How do you feel?"

"Honestly?"

"Yeah."

"I feel like that lady in Bride of Frankenstein, you know how I love those old movies, with her hair standing straight up. Like every nerve in my body is exposed and vibrating. Some days it's hard. Hard to look at myself like the first time in years. But I know it's the right thing, and that keeps me going."

Sam smiled at John like a proud parent. "You're growing up, you bastard."

"Is that what this is? Well it sucks as much as I always thought it would."

They both laughed. The waiter took their order and the rain came down harder. The rosebushes outside looked eager to see winter end. John thought how much better they smelled when they were wild, how life affirming.

The food was hot and tasty. John was much more famished than he thought from his rock climbing adventure. It was good to see Sam again.

"I hope you don't mind me asking, John, but have you ever talked to your young lady since I left?"

"No. I mean no I don't mind. Yes, I talked to her once. Total disaster. Ran into her randomly at the hardware store."

"No kidding? Did she ever open that restaurant?"

"Next month."

"Is she still mad at you?"

"I went to her-"

"John."

"Yeah?"

"I'm going to go the rest room. I'll be back."

Sam had the queerest look on his face. Maybe he was jet lagged. Flying 6 hours can really unsettle your innards.

John sipped his water and regarded the roses. He heard a drip-drop sound and looked to see if his glass was leaking. It was coming from behind him. Turning around, he felt adrenaline rush straight to his head.

Carrie was standing behind him soaking wet with the letter clutched in her hand. She looked like she had walked from her house in the rain. The ink was running along with her eyeliner. It looked like she had been crying. John stood up to face her.

"Carrie, I-"

"Shhh. Just shut up."

His mouth hung open. She closed the distance between him and shut his mouth with hers. They remained like that for some time, oblivious to the other people in the restaurant, unaware Sam had paid the check and left.

When Carrie released him and backed away to take a long look at him, John was smiling like the Buddha himself.

"Now, how about you just come home with me?"

There was a break in the rain and the faintest ray of sunlight shone on the roses.

"Yes, Dear."

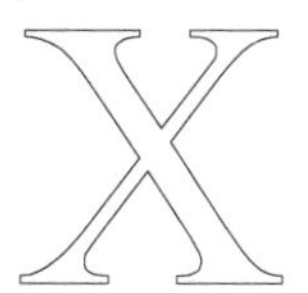

FBI

John woke up smiling in the spreading light of dawn. Carrie fit inside his arms so perfectly, it seemed like design, like puzzle pieces, like the way the laughter of children just made sense to him. He didn't believe in religion, but he believed in loving Carrie. That was enough.

"I see god when I see you." John whispered in her sleeping ear.

The Muse beckoned, but he hit her snooze button. Real artists are creatures of habit. They have routines, methods that work for them on an individual basis. It was challenging for John to tell the Muse to wait a little while.

"It's dawn," she said inside him.

"I'm too comfortable."

"You love painting in this light, it's your favorite."

His toes curled.

"I don't have any brushes here."

"Remember that time, you were hiking in the woods? You had your paints but no brush, so you took a drinking straw you found on the ground and stuffed some shredded napkin in one end. Remember how pleased you were?"

John's hand twitched.

"I'll get a job. I'll stop painting."

"Bullshit," said the Muse.

John shifted his weight, carefully sliding his arm out from under Carrie. She moaned softly and continued dreaming. He covered her carefully with the comforter and took out the heavy duty paper art pad under her desk.

In his mind he took an inventory of the acrylic and oil paints, colored pencils, cheap brushes and pastels available to him in her little box of supplies. The paints weren't the best quality, letting John know how spoiled he had become.

"I will not paint dolphins, not if my life depends on it. I will die first."

It felt right to hold onto some of his prejudices. If he turned into Mother Teresa herself, he still would despise tourist art, and condemn its perpetrators to Purgatory, if not Hell.

John delicately pulled back the comforter from Carrie's naked body. She moved her arm but did not wake. He quickly sketched her, paying special attention to the curves of her body and the folds of the sheet beneath her, revealing a kind of symbiotic flow between them.

Covering Carrie up carefully, he set the pad on the desk and began to work. John had a way of bringing out hues in his flesh tones that rendered his subjects extremely lifelike. As a young artist he had grown bored with the techniques that had been so easy for him to master. He had shied away from using his strengths in favor of experiment, until the day he realized, it was his birthright to do certain things better than anyone else.

Her lips and her breasts looked so inviting, he was falling in love with his work over and over. John wanted the whole world to see her through his eyes. Nudes were out of fashion, and that made John smile. He decided then and there to do a whole show of just nudes of Carrie. Of course he would have to ask her permission. Maybe he could not tell her they would be exhibited until after.

John was smirking to himself when Carrie opened her eyes. She blinked at him and looked at the clock.

"What time is it, John?"

"6:30"

"Oh, too early. Come back to bed you obsessive-compulsive crazy-man. Can't you see I'm naked?"

"I see. Look." John showed her the painting. She smiled and looked at John with pride.

"It's beautiful, John. Come back to bed. Touch me with your hands."

They made love for the 4th time since getting into Carrie's bed. That wasn't counting the bathroom, and the kitchen in the middle of the night when they went looking for a snack.

John was back at his apartment sketching away ideas for more nudes. He strutted around the place like a feather in the wind. His ideas flowed from thought to hand to brush to canvas. This was painting as mania.

His twitching ear told him once more to check the door. John thought it might be the priest or Sam stopping by. What actually greeted him were three pairs of dark sunglasses, six pairs of standard black shoes, and a gaunt almost seven foot tall man with a badge.

"Oh, shit." John thought.

"Mr. Silverthorne?"

"Yes."

"Adam Hatch, Federal Bureau of Investigation. We'd like to ask you a few questions, do you mind if we come in?"

John's heart was racing, and his mind was conjuring up cellmates with names like 'Tiny' and 'Little John'.

"Mr. Silverthorne, may we come in?"

Snapping out of his daydream nightmare, he ushered them in.

"You have no chairs?"

John looked around stupidly. He heard sentences but didn't comprehend their meanings.

"Are you feeling alright today, Mr. Silverthorne?"

"Who the fuck is this giant string bean in my apartment?" John thought. The man's arms were long and skinny like the rest of his body, and John began to see him as a preying mantis. He began to see himself and the whole scene from outside of his body. Yes, this was where one could analyze or at least better observe what was happening. No pain out here.

"Mr. Silverthorne, are you under the influence of psychotropic drugs of any kind?" John snapped back into his body at the mention of drugs.

"No. I'm sorry." He coughed like people often do when someone walks in on them masturbating. It was a way of getting the eyes to focus on one's mouth instead of the genitals. "I'm sorry, I haven't been feeling too good today. Sorry I have no chairs or couch. I just…moved in a few months ago and haven't had a chance. You see, I paint all the time-"

"Mr. Silverthorne, we have plenty of information about your habits. You don't have to apologize, we can stand. We just want to ask you a few questions about the History Repeats No More foundation and its founder Ted Moobakfle."

"Oh." John felt his adrenal glands relaxing. They weren't after him, they wanted Ted. Well, they could have him.

"How long have you known Ted Moobakfle and what is the nature of your relationship to H.R.N.M.?"

"I got a letter a few weeks ago inviting me to a party. I only met him once."

"Are you a financial contributor or do you contribute to the organizations literature with original prose or political ideology?"

"Fuck no. I mean, no, officer-"

"Agent. Agent Hatch."

"No, Agent Hatch. I never met those people before the party and I haven't given them any money."

Agent Hatch pulled a pamphlet from his coat pocket and handed it to John. It was an H.R.N.M. brochure with Apocalypse Fruit Basket on the cover. Underneath the picture was a blurb: Art by John Silverthorne.

"Oh. He asked me if he could use the image of one of my paintings. Ted said they were an environmental group concerned with teaching people better ways to farm."

"Is that what he told you?" Agent Hatch was clearly skeptical. "What prompted you to agree to let him use the image?"

"I thought it sounded like a good cause. I don't know. I wanted to do something charitable."

"Mr. Silverthorne, do you consider yourself a political, or more importantly an environmental activist?"

"No. Not at all. I hate politics."

"Hate, huh? Do you hate them to the point of taking the law into your own hands?"

"Whoa, whoa, where are you going with this? I don't know those people, I don't even vote."

"Standard questioning, Mr. Silverthorne. Nothing personal. Are you a member of the communist party or any anarchist groups?"

"Hell no."

"Do you regularly attend church services? Would you consider yourself religious?"

"No, but c'mon. A lot of religious people turn out to be more nuts than the nuts."

"Our agency has found people who attend church are 50% less likely to engage in acts of domestic terrorism."

"Domestic what?"

"Domestic Terrorism. Mr. Silverthorne do you have any affiliation with the Earth Liberation Front?"

"Who the hell is that? No, and no."

"Ted Moobakfle recently jumped bail on charges of suspected arson. We have reason to believe he is part of an ELF cell. ELF is number one on the United States Domestic Terrorism List. These self-righteous environmental zealots typically blow up or set fire to logging facilities, animal testing labs, or SUV dealerships. Though they claim to be proud of not harming humans in their terrorist acts, they have caused billions of dollars in damage over the years." John shook his head.

"And you think Ted is part of this group?"

"The house he lived in, the one you were seen at by ten eyewitnesses, burned up two weeks ago. In the debris of the house, a compound residue was found that matched the structure fire at a toll-road construction site from 6 months ago. By the time the match came up, Mr. Moobakfle had jumped bail and vanished. Have you been contacted by him in the last week?"

"No."

"We have your phone records. An incoming call from a payphone near Mr. Moobakfle's last whereabouts came in on Wednesday. Your answering machine picked it up and he left no message."

"How do you know it was him?"

"What is most probable usually turns out to be the way things are." John really wanted them to leave.

"So how can I help you?"

"We know you haven't talked to him, we've been following you. Here's my card." It had the FBI seal on it and several phone numbers. "If he calls try to keep him on the phone so we can trace him. We have your phone tapped. And don't think he isn't dangerous. You never know with these fanatics. They are very hard to spot, very sneaky. An ELF cell is almost impossible to detect."

"Why's that?"

"Because they only operate in autonomous groups of 3, making them almost impossible to infiltrate, and arrest." John didn't know what else to say.

"Well I hope you find that Ted. I'll call my agent and tell him to get those people to stop using my artwork."

"That would be a smart move, Mr. Silverthorne." John walked them to the door.

"By the way, his real name isn't Ted Moobakfle."

"It isn't?"

"No. We think it's Felix something, but his past is shrouded in mystery. If you read Moobakfle backwards it says: ELF KABOOM!" Agent Hatch made the hand motions for an explosion for emphasis. He had the slender fingers of an artist. John thought he must hate his job. It was a relief to close the door.

John found Mr. Z.'s phone number and dialed. He listened to that peculiar East Coast New York ring as he waited.

"Hello?"

"Mr. Zamensky?"

"Yes, John? It's about time you called me back. We have to go over your schedule."

"Right, right, I know. Listen, the FBI was just here."

"FBI? What did you do?"

"Nothing, it wasn't me, it's those people I mentioned. The H.R.N.M. It turns out they are domestic terrorists. Can you make sure they don't use my artwork anymore?"

"Domestic Terrorists. Christ on the cross. Done. Anything else? Are you doing okay?"

"Yes. I couldn't be better. I've got a whole new series I'm working on. Nudes."

"Nudes? Hmmm. Mail me some prints and we'll talk about it. Meanwhile you've got that show on the 12th."

"I know. I'm ready for it."

"Great. I'll email you some more information today."

"Thanks, Z."

"Don't mention it, kid. Keep up the good work. This "Flash of Light" series is wonderful!"

Carrie was all smiles. She sat at a window table in her not yet open brewery and sighed. Her father came in with various supplies. He looked at her and knew, just knew what was going on.

"I got ice."

"Oh, Dad, you didn't have to get ice. The ice machine came today. We just plugged it in."

"What, you can't use this ice? Ice is ice. I'll just dump it in the bin."

"Thanks, Dad." She practically danced into the kitchen.

"Nice to see you so jovial today. Who's the lucky guy?" Carrie blushed. Her secret was out.

"John."

"The painter?"

"Yes, that's him."

Her father wasn't sure if he should proceed or drop the subject. He found the less he knew, the better off he seemed to be. Sleeping with a head full of information was difficult at his age. He preferred to let things come to him on a need-to-know basis.

"Dad, please don't tell Mom. She'll tell Grandma and I don't want to hear another lecture."

"She won't hear it from me, Carrie. I don't want to hear it from her either. You're an adult, free to make your own choices and experience the consequences, good or bad."

"Thanks, Dad."

"Except when it comes to this business. As cosigner, we are a team on this until you pay back the loan."

"Right."

She kissed him on the cheek. Carrie had always had her way with him. He couldn't say no to his little girl. Not in a million years.

John painted all day and lit candles when the sun went down. He was one with his brush. His thoughts flowed freely, his movements were fluid, the colors vivid. His composition took on a Neoclassical feel. There were elements of Leonardo, Donatello, Bodacelli, and Michelangelo mixed with found art and Francis Bacon backgrounds. And Carrie's naked body was like sculpture. Was it Neoclassical Postmodern Romanticism?

It was like when God smoked a joint and made the platypus.

"Figure this one out, hee, hee."

John was giddy like a dog in a chicken coop. If he had a tail it would be wagging, tongue drooling, and smiling gleefully.

With glue he applied some real oak leaves to the piece he was working on. Then he sprayed a special chemical he picked up at an antiquing store that would supposedly mummify them and keep them from decomposing.

"Label me will they. This is organic. No, techno-organic. Ha."

John was satisfied. Leaves, barbed wire, metal rings and other found objects infused otherwise negative space with life. He'd seen other people experiment in this way, but most of them cluttered up their work. John's aesthetic ideals kept the theme in the forefront and the window dressing where it belonged.

"Stupid phone."

John froze in mid-stride.

"Better not be that bastard."

He picked up the receiver.

"John Silverthorne here."

"Johnny?"

"Aunt Lucy?"

"Hi, Johnny. I have some bad news for you."

John felt his blood run cold.

"You're Mom is in the hospital. The Doctors don't know if she's going to make it."

He sank to his knees.

"Can you come, can you come to the hospital, Johnny? Don't you think you ought to…make your peace?"

Again he was watching himself from outside. He concentrated and came back.

"Yes. I'll book a flight right away. Where's she at?"

"St. Mary of Magdala Hospital, downtown."

"I'll call you when I get in. Thanks for calling."

John hung up and sat down on the floor. The room was spinning slightly so he lay down to take a nap. There were some things that could be put off for only so long.

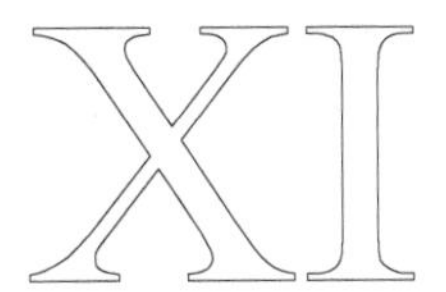

LSD

Coming into Grand Rapids, the plane finally stopped shaking at lower altitude. It was that gray, slushy, transitional time of year when Winter wasn't quite through killing off the suicidal, and Spring wasn't quite ready to melt all the ice. Most of the snow was gone. Grass patches had a strong hold, still green after being deprived of light for four and a half months.

John looked out his window at the land divided into large squares. He wasn't sure if the world from this altitude was better or worse. Life wasn't a series of neat squares in his experience. Each situation might come at him in a neat frame, but he was constantly spilling outside the lines, emotionally, physically. It all went back to kindergarten.

"Color inside the lines, Johnny."

He was 5 and a half and the kid next to him was eating his green crayon.

"I don't like these lines."

The teacher smelled funny to John. He found himself holding his breath whenever she got close. She looked like a fake person, her black hair was cut too perfect. Any minute she would transform into something out of his vampire nightmares.

"What do you mean you don't like the lines?"

She leaned over him and he stopped breathing. He was going to throw up if she didn't go away. His face was turning red.

"I don't like them!" He yelled.

"Johnny, go to the principal's office. We do not yell in class."

John was afraid walking down the hallway to the office. He had wanted to just run out the doors. Run away and never come back.

The fear of not knowing what lay in the Principal's office was soon deflated when he told John to bend over. Now this was something he was used to. Adults had been hitting him his whole life. Why would school be any different? He had been so relieved, he almost forgot to cry. Give them what they want. That was an early lesson. Make them think it hurts. Don't show your real feelings. One time he slipped and let it show in his eyes. He remembered the mockery in his Mother's voice.

"Look at his eyes. Look how mad he is."

When John got bigger, he wouldn't have to take it from them anymore. He could leave at last. All he wanted was to get away from their hands and belts and alcohol breath. The yelling he could stand. He had long since stopped caring what they had to say, stopped feeling the sting of being called every demeaning profanity they could muster. Just make the hands stop. The hands were everywhere.

The plane touched down and his reverie ended. 6 hours in the sky and John felt no more prepared then when he started. His Mother was in the hospital. Maybe dying. It had been so many years since he had seen her. What did she look like? Was her hair gray? The threads of a past life in his hands, he exited the stale air of the plane onto the rampway that led into the airport. Was he three hours ahead, three behind?

"Thank you for flying our airline."

Some kind of greeter lady handed him a coupon as he emerged into the airport out of the tunnel. He threw it in the nearest trashcan as he walked past the baggage claim. John couldn't help but notice the pregnant swollen bellies of the men and the enormous buttocks and thighs of the women. Everyone around him looked like they were counting the days until a heart attack. This was the Midwest he remembered.

The rental car was easy enough to find. It smelled clean and had a cassette player as John had requested. From a black duffle bag, he retrieved a mixed cassette Carrie had made and put it in.

"...Cease to resist, giving my goodbyes..."

Carrie was the only woman he knew who loved that song as much as him. This was the slow version. It fit his mood.

Driving through Grand Rapids, John took in the view of the many church spires, cathedrals, and temples. The city was nicknamed New Jerusalem for a good reason. There were so many churches, he wondered why they needed houses. It seemed this town couldn't agree on anything.

For John it was a town of outward piety and inner decay. His family and the families of his friends were filled with alcoholism, drug abuse, incest, and molestation. Maybe when sin and the devil were constantly being driven down the people's throats, they had no other script to follow when the quiet gnawing horror of their discontent left them sleepless, dreamless.

A light rain left the sky a dull gray. The wipers made a swishing sound, and the heat felt good on his boots. The hospital was straight ahead. Was it the one that had killed his old man? He couldn't remember. The dull brown exterior made him think of a factory. California hospitals looked like office buildings, indistinguishable from banks and law firms. In Michigan, death was right around the corner even from the outside.

After a brief exchange with the nurse, who looked none too healthy, he took the elevator to the intensive care unit.

"I remember this," He said to himself.

The smell of death was so familiar. At 30 years of age, John could tick off over 30 people from his life that were now buried or ash scattered in a field or upon the sea. He felt like the veteran of a war that had been fought on the battlefield of the decaying American Dream.

No less than five fathers on his block had fallen young to heart attacks, including the man who raised him. They had all believed in the Protestant work ethic, all heavy drinkers.

"You're just a number in this world, Johnny. I met the owner of the company today. Been working there twenty years. The guy shook my hand and didn't even know my name. You're just a number."

Looking back, John realized his stepfather revealed the secrets of life in those moments of sad humor. His policy was children should be seen and not heard. John was always incurring the wrath, the beatings, his energy too much to be contained or kept quiet. Eventually he had started drawing.

The hands were so familiar to him. He was always watching for the back of the old man's hand coming at him. John knew every vein and knuckle. The inside was coarse, a welder's hand. The skin slightly cooked on both sides. John had started drawing those hands and the hands of his mother. When they discovered his talent they bought him sketchpads. Drawing was his comfort during many long sentences served in his room for a multitude of transgressions.

At least they hadn't believed in religion. The old man had never lied to John.

"Do you believe in God?"

Putting the beer down, he had stretched out his hand.

"I've been in Vietnam. In places so dark I couldn't see my own hand in front of my face. When your in a darkness like that, you've got to believe in something."

John felt a tremendous sadness with this memory. He couldn't grasp the full meaning at the time. Now he thought he had an idea of what darkness was.

His mother lay before him with a breathing tube in her nose. She was thin, her face gaunt. At the top of the five feet and 1 inch of her was black hair. John knew it was dye. Her real hair was a red brown like his. She had been teased when she was young and her hair was even redder.

"Ma?"

John's voice was barely audible. He hadn't said the word in a long time.

"Ma?"

They told him she was in a coma from some kind of adverse reaction to medication. She might come out of it at any time, or she might die.

John remembered his grandfather being perhaps in this same hospital, in a coma. His mom, her brother, and John stood beside his grandfather's bed. His uncle Paul simply said "Dad?" and John's grandfather sat right up, wide-awake. It was a miracle, or not his time. John thought it was worth a try.

"Ma?"

She didn't move. Just the soft sound of her breathing offered proof of life. John had never seen his mother so thin and frail. A helpless feeling ached in his bones. After an hour of sitting he left flowers on the nightstand and drove to his motel.

John tried to call Carrie, but she wasn't home. There were few things that made John feel lonelier than motels. They were small and desperate places where the worst elements of a city took refuge in drugs and prostitution. He turned the television up to try to mask the sound of yelling and banging.

"I can't stay here."

His throat felt tight and his mind raced. John took a deep breath and tried to remember a phone number from another time. He dialed desperately.

"Hello?"

"Hi. I'm trying to reach Randall."

"What?" There was loud music coming through the phone.

"Randall?"

"Yeah. Who's this?"

"It's John. John Silverthorne."

"John? Oh my god, how are you? Where are you?"

"I'm in town and, hey do you think I could crash on your couch?"

"Come on over, man. I'm having a party. Ike's here, and Smitten, and Raven. I won't tell them you're coming. It'll be a surprise."

"Okay, I'll be there soon."

"Cool."

John couldn't get over his friend's Michigan accent. He had never talked like them, being born in New Jersey, and living in Arizona and Washington. California was just the latest spin on his dialect.

John checked out of the hotel happy to sacrifice the non-refundable fee. He left behind hookers and cokeheads and one-way streets where a left turn was permitted on a red light.

This is where his mom had chosen to live all these years. Cocaine had destroyed her life and taken everything after her husband died. The pack she ran with called themselves the "Westsiders". It was from these barflies that she chose her romantic entanglements. They always beat her up in the end. One surly boyfriend even poured gasoline on her but was arrested before ignition.

John hated them all. He felt so much anger for them, for his mom, for his inability to make things right. The anxiety abated as the city grew smaller in the rearview mirror.

John drove to his old house and parked on the street. He just wanted to see if his old tree was still there. Even at night it was magnificent, the tallest maple around. Countless happy memories of sitting in that tree came back with a flood of tears. It was his oldest friend.

Bare winter branches reached up trying to grasp the Moon. John took out his sketchpad and copied it with meticulous detail. His childhood love guided his hand and he smiled.

"I will make you immortal," he said to the tree. It was the last thing left of his childhood.

Randall's street was lined with cars. John wondered what he was walking into. A man walked by that looked familiar. It dawned on him that everyone he used to know was probably inside the house.

"I could sleep in the car," he sighed.

John put on his bravest face and entered the maelstrom. Right away Randall saw him and came charging up, lifting John in a big gear hug. Several vertebrae popped into place.

"Johnny!"

"Hey Randall. Good to see you."

"This is great. Let me get you a beer."

"Uh-"

He put a beer in John's hand and practically dragged him into the living room. Randall turned down the stereo.

"Attention, everyone! Tonight's honored guest has arrived- John Silverthorne!"

The music roared back to life. A couple familiar faces appeared. John squinted at first. Then he realized what was awkwardly obvious. Everyone he had known had gotten fat and old. A girl he had asked out and been rejected by so long ago reiterated this fact.

"John! You look the same as you did in High School. God, you haven't changed."

"Uh, thanks. You look great, too," he lied.

"What have you been up to?"

John hadn't opened his beer, but he could tell it was going to be a night of conversations he didn't want to have. He opened the can of light American swill and swallowed hard.

"I've been painting."

"Oh, my brother is a painter. He's painting some condominiums over on Baldwin this week."

"Good for him." John sighed and took a bigger swallow.

Carrie looked out her window forlorn and lonely. The street was tranquil and the Sun was setting. She felt a melancholy mood she couldn't explain.

John hadn't called or if he had he hadn't left a message. She couldn't understand a lot of his little personality quirks. What was wrong with answering machines? How was she supposed to know he called? Didn't he miss her? Was she being too much of a woman thinking he should drop everything and call his girlfriend?

Jane was laughing in the kitchen. Carrie could hear other voices, and the sound of the coffee maker. Coffee sounded good. She put her hair back and went downstairs.

In the kitchen with Jane were her boyfriend and another man.

"Hi Carrie. We're making coffee."

"I smelled it."

"This is Mike's friend Jim."

A tall guy with black hair shook her hand. He resembled an actor who used to play teenage heartthrobs but had grown up. He had the straight teeth of a model. Carrie didn't mean to, but the picture of him as one of those underwear models went through her mind.

"Nice to meet you," he said.

Jane handed Carrie a cup of coffee.

"Carrie is opening a brewery in just a couple of weeks."

"Where at?" asked Jim.

Carrie lowered her cup.

"Downtown."

"What inspired you to open a brewery?"

"I've been making beer since I was a teenager, and it seemed like the next logical thing to do."

"Are you going to have big screen t.v.s for people to watch sports on?"

"No. It's also going to be a restaurant and who wants to watch television while they're eating?"

"I like to watch the news sometimes during dinner."

"I don't watch t.v."

Carrie was tiring of this conversation. Where was John?

"I like to catch up on world events when I get home from the yacht company."

"You work on boats?"

"My father owns the company. I help manage it. Some of my friends think I'm too young to have such a serious job, but I enjoy it."

"Sounds wonderful."

Carrie gave Jane a desperate look.

"Carrie will you come with me to the bathroom a minute? Excuse us boys, we have to powder our noses."

Mike and Jim laughed and compared sports statistics.

John was at the kitchen table with Randall and two skinny blonde girls, Cindy and Mindy. The party was raging inside and outside the house. John finished beer number seven and felt his face getting numb with alcohol. Cindy passed around a tin that might have held mints. When it got to John he saw only little squares of paper smaller than his pinky fingernail.

"What the hell is this?"

"It's LSD. Eat it." Mindy said.

John looked at Randall. Randall shrugged and stuck out his tongue. A square of the paper was slowly dissolving.

"C'mon John," said Cindy. "You're with your old friends, have fun."

"Fun." John said distantly. He put a square in his mouth and swallowed a mouthful of beer.

30 minutes later petaled glorious energy shot up his spine and he felt another in a long line of out of body experiences. This time he actually imagined himself split in to two bodies. It was excruciatingly painful to be in two places at once. He tried touching his four hands together and snapped back into one body with a painful shock.

John took a deep breath and looked around the living room. In each face he found each person's life story open and careening down a slide laughing like a five year old, an old fashioned metal playground slide that connected from their foreheads to John's. It was like reading a diary at light speed without meaning to. That woman in the corner was unhappy because she had never been in love. And that man by the stereo thinks about killing himself every Christmas when he is alone. They just kept coming, slamming into John's mind, like bumper cars, unexpected heavy slaps on the back. He felt the impact and saw greens and reds, blues and yellows like spider webs connecting everyone. It was overwhelming and emotionally painful, didn't fit with the good feeling in his body, and he was beginning to split apart again, but didn't want to.

With great effort he moved himself outside into the backyard. He was alone standing in the damp ground. An isolated patch of hard snow that hadn't let go, hadn't surrendered to the sun, formed a ring around a pine tree. John approached the tree with his hand extended. The porch lights let him see the tree as bright as day. The bark was more intricate than anything in his experience. It had to be the drug. This was vision beyond 20/20 and the canyons and cliffs, secret languages, and holes to other worlds upon the bark hypnotized him.

John must've been looking too hard because he began to see the sap flowing beneath the bark. From the tips of the branches to exposed roots below the snow ring, a vast series of canals and rivers, tributaries and nerve-like nexuses reveled themselves. Time lost all meaning. John might have been standing there for an hour, maybe only a minute.

He tried to count to 60, but couldn't make it past 7 or 8 without being distracted by the sound of the wind. To a person whose senses had always been so vivid, the LSD was almost violent in its amplified presentation, no, demand, that he should see colors, smell earth, feel textures, and hear nature like a collision of worlds. Everything was piercing him like knives, one minute joyfully the next making him cry.

Inside the bathroom, he stared at the mirror. His face changed into his father's, then his grandfather's, then a marble bust. John closed his eyes for what felt like an hour.

When he opened them he saw a 7-foot tall hawk-headed man standing in front of him. He was in a white room, deep underground. The hawk man placed a beaded breastplate over John's head that covered his chest and back. It was painted red with plant dye or blood. With his magnificently huge arm he pointed for John to exit the cave through a carved hole.

John emerged into a forest with trees higher than anything he had ever seen. They seemed to go up forever. A green-breasted hummingbird zipped past him and then landed on his shoulder.

"Where am I?"

"This is the forest of those who choose to build trees," the bird said. John loved the soft light that bathed this pleasant place.

"How do you build a tree?"

The hummingbird smiled. It beat its wings and circled his head three times before landing again on his shoulder.

"You don't have to spend your life in reaction, John. When the world acts upon you, if you choose to let it go by, and instead of reacting act for your own reasons, then you begin building a tree."

John wondered if he was dead.

"This is your tree."

A tall chestnut brown tree stretched its limbs high out of sight. He felt the tree with his hand, pushing gently. It was sturdy and felt warm to the touch.

The bathroom door burst open and the forest vanished as John opened his eyes for real.

"John, are you okay? You've been gone for hours." It was Randall with a beer in each hand.

"I don't know man. That acid is hitting me pretty hard. I just had a strange dream. I was talking to birds."

"You need to keep drinking, John. Regulate the trip, you know. We dropped hours ago and you're going to start peaking. You want to drink in case it gets too intense."

Randall's face had become see-through like the tree in the backyard. John could see the bones of his face and head.

"Randall, I'm not a doctor, and I've never taken anatomy…but I can see every bone in your body."

"Cool. Take this beer, man. Mellow. Mell-low."

John took the beer and slammed it. He almost tripped over a couple making out in the hallway. There was a bottle of Captain Morgan on the kitchen counter. The music and the voices made John want to curl in a ball and disappear, but he forced himself to the rum. There was a green flight jacket on the chair closest to him. He put it on and went outside holding the Captain Morgan in his hand like a life preserver.

"Why did I do this? Why did I do this?" he sighed.

Each thought bloomed like time-lapse photography of frost on a window, that instantly spread out in an intricate pattern of a hundred other thoughts. He took a shot from the bottle. They kept coming until it hit him.

John took the LSD because he knew with his mind out of control, there was no avoiding himself or his deepest darkest feelings and demons. There was no escaping into other personas, no justifying anything in the kaleidoscope collage of his raw feeling. The Captain Morgan was sweet, but he couldn't look at the Captain's face, for fear he would start talking.

John went walking with no idea what time it was or fear of drinking in public. The cold air was the only normal sensation he recognized, and he cherished it. He saw a porch of an industrial building that was in the shadows removed from the road. It looked like a nice place to sit.

"I've got to get control of this," he said to the concrete steps. A voice in his head told him to let go. There was a payphone across the parking lot.

After 15 minutes that felt like eternity a taxi picked John up.

"Hey buddy, you can't bring that bottle in my cab."

John looked at the cab then looked at the bottle. Somehow the cabbie knew this man in this deserted parking lot in the middle of the night would rather walk to China with that bottle then ride to the next block without it.

"Never mind. It's all right. Get in."

John was glad to take some direction. He couldn't trust his own mind. The peak had been going for a while already. He just had to make it to the other side and everything would mellow out. Could be 30 minutes, could be 2 hours.

"Mell-low." He said to himself after taking a swig of Captain.

"Where do you want to go, or should I pick a place?" John became vexed.

"Why do you say that? Are you my guide?"

The cabbie didn't find that an unusual question, at least from out-of-towners. This guy was definitely from somewhere else.

"Do you want to go to a bar?"

"No. The hospital."

"You okay?"

It was hard to push aside the multiple conversations he was having with himself to utter the normal replies required in a dialogue. "Fine. My mom is there."

"Which hospital?"

John took another sip. "Mary Magdalene."

"Got it. You want a smoke?"

"Do…You…Want…A…Cigarette?"

"Yes." John laughed, realizing what he was putting the cabbie through. He wanted to tell him he was on LSD and he would be fine in a little while, but that was way too much to put into words.

Carrie lay in bed alone and missing John. She wrapped her arms around herself and imagined holding his warm body.

Her thoughts were anxious ones, coming at her like the run on sentence from hell. There was a knock on her door.

"You okay, kid?" It was Jane checking up on her.

"I guess so. Can't sleep. I miss John."

"Aw. Don't worry, he'll be back."

"What if he has to stay for months, or doesn't come back. Or he meets someone else, or decides he doesn't want to be with me?"

"Shhh. Calm down. He'd be crazy not to come back to you. What, is he going to fall for some farmer's daughter?"

Carrie frowned.

"Kidding. I hear the girls in Michigan are really ugly. They have beards. Some have four beards."

Carrie laughed in spite of herself. Jane tucked her in and closed the door. Falling off to sleep, she dreamed of humans with bird heads.

John stepped out of the cab and lit the cabbie's last cigarette. John looked at the arches of the doors, modeled after cathedral arches. He recalled his art history teacher…

"The arched entrance to the famous cathedrals is a symbol of the vagina. This further illustrated by the clitoral flower placed above the peak of each famous archway. Man is reentering the womb and making the long walk up the birth canal to submit himself to the divine in the symbolic place of conception."

His mother was inside. John had to traverse this womb to get to his mother. He felt like a tragic mythological figure. Inside was not his mother, but the Minotaur.

"Oh, god. I shouldn't have thought that."

The gray walls of the hallways became stone, and the darkness coming through the few windows was the dark of the labyrinth. He had to find Ariadne and the golden thread if he wanted to make it out alive.

John avoided the night nurse, sneaking past as her back was turned. The elevator took him to the 13th floor. He didn't remember elevators having a 13th floor. Maybe it was the drug.

Lying in the dark was his mother. There was a little more color in her cheeks, probably from the intravenous feeding tube. John grabbed an old brown chair and stared at the enigma of his past. He pulled the chair closer to her bed, stopping halfway worried the noise would wake someone.

"Everyone's in a coma, stupid." He was trying so hard not to freak out. "Ma?"

She didn't stir. He talked very quietly, forgetting again that no one was likely to hear.

"Ma, I've got to tell you something." Her face kept threatening to change shape, but John held it in check somehow.

"I want you to know, all these years you've been doing drugs and drinking, and letting these drunks beat you…I know you've been punishing yourself because he died and you lived. You feel guilty. I want you to know I understand. I have felt the same guilt for so long. Why am I still here? All the people we've buried, Ma…some so young, some old, some real good people who never had a malicious bone in their body. I don't know why they had to die. But that's not important, Ma. We shouldn't feel guilty that we're here. We should make the most of our time."

His mind started to wander off contemplating the mystery of time with the voice of a famous narrator, but he managed to pull it back.

"If you die now, Ma. I want you to know, I forgive you. For everything. If you get through this, and you continue to live the way you've been living these 17 years since he died, I still forgive you. I love you either way. And I'll always be your kid."

John's mother continued her soft breathing, but otherwise didn't stir. He put the chair back where he had found it. The elevator down was like a descent into a coal mine. The door finally opened. There were no canaries.

"Sir, can I help you? Visiting hours are closed, sir."

The night nurse had him.

"I am just leaving. Thank you. Thank you."

To his own ears he sounded like Ed Sullivan.

Back in the cold night air, John walked down the block trying to find a liquor store to buy cigarettes. A couple drops of cold rain came down. He quickened his pace.

"I want this to end now. Anytime would be fine."

The sky answered with a downpour and thunder.

"Shit."

The rain pelted him and he realized he wasn't out of the peak yet. Each drop felt like it was penetrating him, melting him like a sand castle washed out by a wave.

"I'm melting. That's crazy. People can't melt."

John felt his adrenal glands pumping rocket fuel. This was panic. This was terror. This was…silly.

He giggled. Deep within him a song was playing, a very little song. Something about taking an amount of love out of life equal to the love you bother to make.

John's stomach was filled with golden light and he felt the fear vanish. There was something inside him he had never realized. In his mind it was a megalithic structure, a foundation made of giant blocks. The blocks were the wonder, awe, and love he felt for nature.

"This is what comes out in my art!"

The rain stopped as quickly as it came. At least it seemed that way. There was no way to measure time on LSD. John knew he could've been walking for hours or minutes.

Either way the peak was subsiding. He was coming down, had emerged from the labyrinth, and had found the golden thread.

The phone rang for the seventh time. Carrie picked it up with her left hand from the bedside table.

"Hello?"

"Hi, Carrie."

"John?" Her eyes opened and she sat up.

"Where are you?"

“On my way home. The airport. I’ll be back tonight.”
“What happened with your mom?”
“She woke up.”
Carrie felt a mountain slide off her back. “Good.”
“I have so much to tell you, Carrie. So much happened I”
“Are you okay John?”
“Yes. I’m great.” John smiled. “I’m great.”

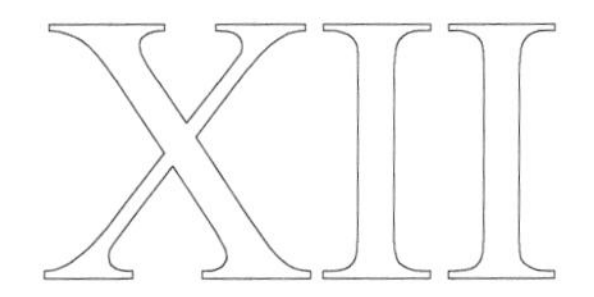

SOUP OR SALAD?

Carrie stood breathlessly at the baggage claim, waiting to see John's familiar boots coming down the stairs from the off limits area. Middle aged men with pregnant bellies that might have held twins or triplets smiled at her as they walked by. Their wives had little pot roasts of their own in the oven. Carrie tried to imagine her stomach swelling, tried to see herself with a bloated older John. Did these people still make love? How did they get so out of shape? Was the airport always this eye catching? Children cried, pilots headed for the airport bar, bellies swelled under the fluorescent lights, but all the while, Carrie felt a nervous excitement that overpowered her amateur anthropology.

John had only been gone two weeks, but Carrie missed him months. The abrupt shock of sleeping with John every night and then sleeping alone had made Carrie lose 5 pounds, forget to turn off her headlights, burn a whole batch of beer, remember what day of the week it was, buy a new pair of jeans, try drinking herself to sleep, forget what day of the week it was, return a pair of jeans, and share her bed with a stuffed animal.

Before John, Carrie was invincible, enough for herself. This feeling of absence was like a burn on the roof of her mouth. She kept testing it with her tongue, but it was always there. She was busy all day preparing to open the brewery, only to find it waiting in the quiet moments at the end of the day.

Carrie watched for the third time a large throng of people with the faces of insurance salesmen, interior decorators, real estate agents, secretaries, computer programmers, car salesmen, and that kid that got picked on in gym class come down the stairs with no John. Not one of these people looked remotely like an artist. She couldn't help smiling. John thought normal people were crazy, and they thought the same about him.

What was it that made him go his way while most people settled for mediocre lives of quiet desperation? Was it his stubbornness? He had complained to Carrie, or maybe it was bragging, about all the years he spent starving and sleeping on couches. She didn't believe art only came through suffering. That was a cop out for people who couldn't handle the multitasking demanded to have one's life together financially *and* do art. John set Carrie off one day with a comment about suffering.

"Without experiencing life, people make crap art."

"John, life is not all about suffering, do you think that? Are you a Buddhist? I know you enjoy the world in spite of all the things you rail against."

"Yeah. You're right. I'm just glad I was willing to suffer. I knew it would work out in the end."

"John, everything works out in the end, but consider the alternative."

"What do you mean?"

"Consider how much better your life can be if you apply yourself instead of letting everything 'work out'."

John had scratched his goatee.

"I wish you had been around to tell me that when I was 18. Would've saved me a lot of grief."

Carrie suspected Georgia O'Keefe had simply loved vaginas, enthralled with the labia and clitoris, and all the wonders of the vulva. She painted flowers joyfully. Life was not suffering in the kingdom of the flowers of Georgia O'Keefe. Life was vivid and throbbing, engorged and opening like a rose.

Carrie leapt up from the wall she had been sitting against. John was coming down the stairs, grinning like a boy with a secret to keep. Reaching the bottom of the stairs, they were upon each other in a few quick strides.

John picked her up and swung her around. They kissed for at least a minute with their eyes closed. Nothing mattered so much as that moment. Finally, John spoke.

"I brought you something!" John reached in the pocket of his green jacket. He was smiling foolishly. "This is great." He kept digging.

At last his hand emerged with a brown lump. John placed it in Carrie's hand. She looked at it queerly. Was it hashish? Mud? A brick of sea monkeys that would come to life in water?

"Read the label."

"Mackinaw Island Fudge. Oh. Fudge. Thank you."

John put his arm around her and they went to pick his bag off the conveyor belt.

"Airports are such unpredictable quagmires." John remarked.

"What do you mean?"

"You never know how long you will wait to check in, to board, to leave. Then they can lose your luggage, ground your flight, take you in the back room and search you for drugs when you're 14 and on your way home from Jamaica. One fat guy gleefully puts on a rubber glove and you clench your butt cheeks hard and look for a window."

"I have no response to that."

"I predict in the future, people will take virtual vacations, strapped into their home computers, living inside a simulation for two weeks. Of course, the fun thing for hackers will be to write in code for an airport experience from hell."

"Is this how you amuse yourself during a 6 hour flight? Thinking up these scenarios?"

"Yeah. Pretty much."

"I am never strapping myself into a virtual vacation, Mr. You and I are just gonna deal with the airport. You got that?"

"Yes, dear."

"There's your bag."

They left the chaos of the airport and set out for Laguna Beach, where the more subtle moments before sunset revealed the sea in an opal light. John knew he couldn't do it justice with his brush. Nature was still his favorite painter.

It was Carrie's dad who suggested she have the grand opening for the Georgia O'Keefe Brewery at night on a Thursday. She had butterflies all day. This was her dream, and whatever happened, she would be among those who dare.

"John, bring me the hammer!"

Carrie was standing on a table against the wall that faced the doors. She had a nail between her lips and a framed drawing in her hand. John stopped banging and handed a large hammer to Carrie.

"I thought the drawing you gave me on our first date would look nice here, where the customers walk in."

John regarded the drawing like a forgotten friend. Had he known it was the first thing people would look at upon entering the Georgia O'Keefe Brewery, he would have impishly been more graphic. He thought better of saying so.

"Aw. I'm glad you kept it."

"It was a nice memento of our first date."

John smiled. "I have to confess something though."

"Yes?"

"I don't like red wine."

"I knew that John, by that stupid face you made every time you took a sip."

"Nothing gets past you, does it?"

"Nope."

"How long until people start arriving?"

"About 3 hours." Carrie sighed.

"Want to go to my place?"

"No. I have too much to do. You don't have to stick around though. Just come back at 7."

"Okay. I have some ideas I have to get out. I'll be back."

John removed the last of his nude series from his easels and set up fresh canvas. He liked having 6 pieces going at once in a circle he could walk around. With the 'Flash of Light' series, then the "Nudes', it had been like painting a mural on separated sections. A real collector would easily see the continuity between the nudes and the light. This time, he would go further.

John sketched the tree as he had seen it on LSD. On the next canvas he drew Randall's see-through body, with bony face and muscle detail. He improvised a caged bird, a dog, and a flower with the minutest detailed vein laden petals.

He worked furiously, loosing all track of the outside world. The phone rang, he didn't hear. The old lady who lived below him banged on the ceiling with a broomstick, trying again to get him to turn down his music. John was oblivious.

The paint smell filled the apartment. The series was taking shape, the improvement being that if all 6 pieces were put together, it would be seen that a long boney arm was stretched out in the background. It started in the tree painting, resembling a long strip of blue white ribbon on the ground. By the sixth painting, only the perspicacious eye would see it was not long thin pebbles that cradled a rose. They were the boney fingers of a skeleton hand.

John smiled warmly, quite pleased with himself. Probably no one would figure it out, and it would be an inside joke for him alone. It was fun and that was what mattered to him now.

He noticed the Sun going down and panicked. Racing to the phone, he picked up the handset, and then realized he didn't know the brewery's number.

"Shit."

John dialed Carrie's house. The phone rang and rang.

"Of course no one's there. They're all at the Brewery."

He dialed the operator.

"Operator, may I help you?"

"Can you tell me the time?"

"The number for time is 376-4214. Have a nice day."

"Wait! Hello? Hello?

He gave up and ran out the door.

John arrived breathless in front of the brewery. A long line of well dressed people stood chatting and smoking on the sidewalk. The doors had not yet opened.

Discreetly moving to the back of the building, John entered through the back door of the kitchen.

"Que Paso?"

"Hi."

John emerged into the dining area and saw Carrie spreading white linen tablecloths. She saw John approaching and smiled. He felt relief wash over him.

"I was starting to wonder if you were going to be late."

"No, I uh…was working, but I looked at the clock and-"

"We don't open for thirty minutes, John. It's okay. You told me this morning you need a new clock."

John smiled sheepishly. "Is there anything you need me to do?"

The phone rang before she could answer. Carrie put the last tablecloth on the last uncovered table, and went to the phone on the bar counter.

"Hello? Fever? Flu? I see. Thank you." Carrie hung up and stood motionless at the bar. She seemed to pale for a moment then regained her color.

"What is it?" John asked.

"Come here, John."

John approached the bar, having the feeling of approaching the 'bench' in a courtroom. He knew she was about to confide some privileged information somehow. Outside humid voices pressed upon the windows.

Carrie reached over and set two shot glasses on the counter. John saw her pick up a bottle of expensive Tequila and fill them up the rim without spilling a drop. She looked at him with a calm controlled smile.

"My lead waiter just called in sick. A waitress I hired hasn't shown up." She handed him a shot glass.

"Hold out your hand, John." Carrie poured a little salt on his hand. She placed a lime slice in front of him.

"I am down two servers, and I have no one I can count on to solve this crisis except myself, and you." She poured salt on her own hand and grasped a lime wedge.

"I will take the place of the lead waiter and expediter. I need you to handle a couple tables for me."

John's eyes became wide and big as cow eyes. He felt the panic Carrie wasn't allowing herself to feel spreading up his legs. Did she seriously want him to take orders from Laguna's most affluent citizens and social climbers?

"Carrie, I've never waited tables be-"

"Shhh. It's not that difficult. You smile and say hi. You ask what they would like to drink. When you come back with their drinks, you ask what they want to eat. Then ask if they would like soup or salad, and when the food comes up in the window bring it to them. After three bites or three minutes you check on them. Keep bringing them drinks and when the foods done, give them the bill. Got it?"

"But-"

"Shhh. I need you to do this for me, John. Now is not the time to fall apart. This is opening night at the brewery, and you're going to have to keep it together."

John looked at Carrie and in her eyes he saw the faintest glimmer of doubt. She had never shown weakness in front of John, and he guessed this was as close as she would ever come.

"Okay," he said.

"Okay?"

Wrapping her arm around his, shot glasses in each of their hands, she managed a little smile of faith and sighed.

"Now lick."

They licked the salt off each other's hands.

"Swallow."

John threw back and felt the Tequila setting fire all the way down.

"Suck."

Carrie looked at him with the lime wedge stuck in her mouth and they both giggled.

"Okay, John. Let's do this shit."

The brewery was filled to capacity, every table, every bar stool occupied. Carrie had to keep an eye on legal capacity in case the fire department came to check. There was a thirty-minute wait, and people still clumped on the sidewalk like gum stuck to a shoe.

John was wondering why he gave up smoking, what he possibly could've been thinking was beyond him. He muttered to himself in mimicked voices, on his way to and from picking up the food and his tables. In a cranky old ladies voice he spoke to himself.

"Does the salad have peanuts? I can't have peanuts or…I'll dieeee."

John wished he had peanuts, or maybe just one peanut. He would casually let it fall onto the table as he set the salad down. It would be worth it to see the old bag's expression.

"Carrie, do we have any peanuts?"

Carrie was making a couple salads herself. She looked up quizzically. "Did someone request peanuts on their salad?"

"Not exactly. I thought it might spice it up a little, you know?"

"I don't want to go changing recipe's just yet. Tell them you're sorry but it doesn't come with peanuts."

"Okay."

He looked over at the table and resumed muttering, accenting each syllable.

"I need art-i-fi-cial sweet-en-er for my coff-ee. I have di-a-bee-tes."

Would it really be so bad to eat them when they get old? Less traffic accidents, less hospitals…How many of them were having a good time when they couldn't taste or smell or have sex anymore?

John set the salads down in front of the old lady and her husband, forcing a smile. He noticed the intricate blue-green veins, liver spots, and soft wrinkled flesh of her hands. For a moment, he couldn't stop looking, transfixed like an animal in bright light.

"Young man, are you wondering how we got to be so old?" The lady gave the first hint of a smile.

"I'm sorry. I was looking at your hands. I'm an artist."

"How nice. What kind?"

"What kind? I paint. People mostly. Kind of romantic post-modern."

"You want to paint my hands?"

"I might. Hands are one of my favorite things to draw. It's kind of how I got into art. Hands."

"These old hands have done a lot."

She reached across the table and clasped her husband's hands. His were large, once powerful hands with thick fingers. Arthritis was beginning to gnarl his knuckles.

"I was in the Red Cross in the big war. That's where I met my husband. He was in the army. We owned an antique store after and for many years while we raised our children. They all have children of their own now." She laughed faintly.

"For a long time we traveled Europe, Egypt, South America. Eventually our bodies became too old, too weak, and too dependent on medicine and doctors. But now we have our memories. What's your name?"

"John."

"John, you stick with your art. Get your name out there. Now is the time to take the initiative while you're still young. You don't want to wait tables the rest of your life do you?"

"No, ma'am."

"If you pursue your dream, when you look back you can't regret not trying. That's how you live a good life."

John smiled. He went from wanting to eat them to wanting to adopt them.

"Hey, buddy, is our food ready?"

A rotund man at the table facing John's back was obviously getting ready to eat his children.

"Let me go check," he said over his shoulder. "Excuse me."

At the window John could see the cooks scrambling about the kitchen like summer ants over a fallen chocolate banana. The fat man's food was not ready.

"I already ate my napkin and my spoon. I'm starving to dea-eth."

"John, who are you talking to?"

"Myself."

Carrie gave him an amused smile. "You're doing great. Even with the mess-ups, I haven't had to comp any of your orders, yet."

"And I haven't attacked anyone, not that they don't deserve it."

"Welcome to the restaurant business."

"Everyone likes your beer. Are you happy?"

"I think when the night ends and we close the doors. I will be able to sit down and enjoy it."

John's order came up. "See you there."

Jane and John sat at the bar while Carrie poured from behind the counter, their happy laughter interrupted only by the licking of salt, swallowing of tequila, and lime sucking sounds.

"How much did you make tonight?" John inquired.

"A lot," Carrie grinned and tried to wink at Jane.

"What is that? What is that winky thing you do?" John asked..

"Now, John, you shouldn't make fun of people's disabilities." Jane put her hand on his shoulder seriously

"What?"

"Carrie can't wink her eyes."

"I thought she had an itch or something."

Carrie regarded John coolly. "I'll show you an itch, Mr."

"Sweetheart. You can't wink? That's so cute."

"She's blushing, how precious."

"Shut up. Excuse me a moment, I'm going to the lady's room."

Jane and John watched her go.

"Do you think she's going to practice winking?"

"You better watch yourself," Jane smiled. "You just recently got out of the abyss. You don't want to fall back in so soon."

"The abyss?" John asked.

"Tell me you've never heard of ladder theory."

John shrugged.

"Okay, the basic thing is men have one ladder that every woman they meet goes on, closer to the top or closer to the bottom based on attraction. Women are supposed to have two ladders. One is the 'friend ladder' for guys they only see as friends and one is the 'good' ladder. That means guys they would sleep with placed closer to the top or to the bottom based on attraction, money, etc."

"How come guys don't get a friend ladder?"

"Because guys generally will sleep with anyone, even their 'friends'."

"I see. So what is the abyss?"

"This is where my personal outlook gets involved. I think women have a third ladder."

"And guys still only get one, what a rip-off."

"In the classic theory, once in a while a guy tries to jump ladders. A man high up on the friend ladder may interpret affection and compliments as a sign that he has somehow moved to the 'good' ladder. Most of the time this is not the case, and in jumping he falls in-between into the abyss below."

"Okay, that makes sense. But I was never on Carrie's friend ladder."

"That's true. Which is where my addendum comes in. Women have a third ladder. You were at the top of Carrie's ladder and you blew it. You were a real first class jerk."

John squirmed in his seat a bit.

"I'm not trying to be mean. Just telling it like it is."

"You're right. I was a jerk."

"When you acted like an ass, you fell all the way from the top of the ladder down into the abyss. Or did you?"

"Did I? You just said I did?"

"This is where my addition to the science of ladders explains something the originators didn't think of."

"Which is?"

"Women have a third ladder reserved for the men who they really loved that screwed up. These are the guys they really cared about. And no matter how high a guy might be on the classic 'good' ladder, if she is single, chances are she would rather try again with a man from her third ladder than emotionally invest herself in someone new. Probably fortunately for her, most of these jerks are the types that won't admit they did anything wrong, won't say they're sorry, and don't take responsibility to change for the sake of the relationship. And that John, is where you set yourself apart. You said you were sorry, you admitted wrong, and you showed a willingness to change. Carrie was probably very relieved after all the time and emotion she spent on you that you made the effort to redeem yourself. And that is the only reason I'm talking to you tonight."

"So I should feel good about myself?"

"You should feel like a jerk. But a jerk who wants to be better. Just don't push your luck. I've got my eye on you."

Carrie returned from the restroom.

"What have you two been talking about?"

"John was just telling me how lucky he is to have someone like you. Isn't that sweet."

Carrie almost blushed again, but took control instead.

"Damn straight."

Jane stood up and slung her purse over her shoulder.

"I'll leave you two alone. I have to get up early."

Carrie came around the counter and sat down next to John, leaning her head on his shoulder.

"I'm tired."

"You did good, kid. You did real good."

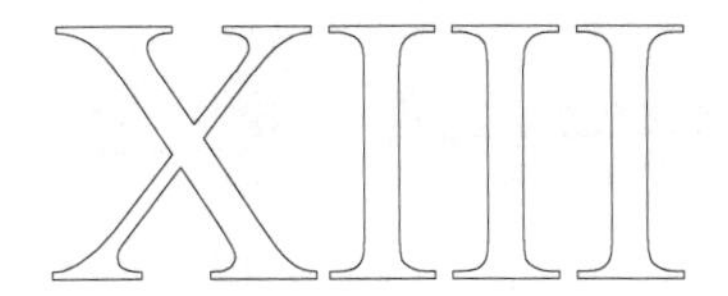

SUBTLE LIKE A T-REX

John woke up slowly in Carrie's bed feeling like a cat in a sunbeam. He reached for her and felt only blanket. His ears perked up. There was a sizzling sound coming from downstairs. His nose caught up with his brain and he smelled pancakes. He put on his clothes in case Jane was home, and went downstairs to the kitchen.

Carrie was flipping flapjacks and humming a melody John faintly recognized. On the counter were two plates, butter, syrup, whip cream, and blueberries. John had come to understand the lady loved her blueberries, and breakfast meant purple lips and coffee. He made a small grocery list in his head for later.

"Good morning." Carrie smiled and pushed a stack of pancakes in front of John.

"Thank you."

She sat down beside him on the couch and clicked on the TV. The news was a habit of hers John was getting used to. It bored him, but the commercials made him laugh and gave him wickedly obscene ideas for painting. He was snoozing in his brain, contentedly chewing away at the warm flapjackety goodness in his mouth, when something caught his eye.

"Turn it up."

Carrie adjusted the volume.

"Police arrested a Mission Viejo man today who is accused of arson in connection to the domestic terrorist group ELF."

A group of police cars pulled up to a courthouse and got out of their cars.

"The man, known only as Felix, was apprehended at an all-vegan restaurant in Irvine. He resisted arrest but was not armed, and continues to proclaim his innocence."

The police pulled a man with long curly brown hair out of the back of a squad car, and led him up the steps of the courthouse. John looked closer and realized it was the kilt wearing man from the Green House.

"That's strange."

"What?"

"I think I forgot to tell you, but I met that guy at a party. The FBI came to my house to ask me if I knew anything. I thought they were after his roommate."

"Bizarre."

In front of the courthouse a spokesmen addressed the press. Unmistakable as a clown at a bar mitzvah, John saw Ted in the crowd facing the camera, grinning like Mephistopheles at Faust's funeral.

"That son of a bitch."

"What? Who?"

"That guy!" John pointed.

"The white guy with the afro?"

"Yeah. He must have set him up."

"Why do you say that?"

"Just a feeling, my love. Just a feeling."

Ted actually waved at the camera and mouthed the classic 'Hi Mom'. John let out a little laugh and clicked off the TV.

"Carrie, do you ever feel like taking on something bigger than yourself. Like maybe you could do something really good for the world, but you don't know what?"

She sipped her coffee. "I feel like my brewery is enough for now. Appreciation for the good things we have is just as important as reaching for the things we don't."

"Still, sometimes I feel like I could do more than just paint. Speaking of painting, I have to get ready for the show tonight. You sure surprised me when you asked me to have it at your restaurant."

"John, if you are going to exhibit nude paintings of me, along with your see-through people, I'd rather have it at my place."

"If you feel uncomfortable, I won't show them."

"No. It's fine. It's flattering. Besides, at a private showing there will hopefully bring people with taste and not just riffraff."

"Hey. I resemble that comment."

"No you don't. You're more like a rough diamond. A little spit and polish and you clean up real nice."

She grinned at John and he pounced upon her, sending blueberries eloping to the unknown country of the couch underside.

John sat at a table while Carrie served her special beers. Conversations flowed easily as people milled around the work.

Carrie wasn't the least embarrassed by her own nude body being on display. She sat down next to John in between serving drinks.

"I like the one with the skeleton fingers holding the rose in the background."

"That's why you're my girl. You appreciate subtlety."

"John, you are about as subtle as a T-Rex. But I like flowers." She squeezed his hand.

John made a show of looking around at the Georgia O'Keefe prints on the walls. "I noticed."

The door opened and a man entered wearing a green felt hat and two long braids of hair coming down his head. His coat was weathered like he had been caught in several downpours. He looked across the room at John and smiled. John couldn't place him.

"Who's that?"

"I don't know."

The man walked around the paintings, especially admiring the one odd piece John had thrown in.

The card on the frame said, "Look in Pot". A haggard looking piece of pottery with fissures and a flakey porous surface sat on a fireplace mantle. The room was dim and dirty. Articles of clothing were strewn about. On the floor were five small chests with lids thrown open. They were empty and a thin bald man was wringing his long boney fingered hands in grief. To the perspicacious eye, there was a faint glow on the lip of the old pot.

The man in the hat laughed loudly, causing a few people to stare. He looked out of place. Maybe European.

He crossed the room to where John and Carrie sat.

"Is this your lady?"

John looked at him closely to see if there was any crazy in his eye.

"I'm Carrie. And you are?"

"Loki. Nice to meet you."

John's face lit up with recognition. He shook the man's hand warmly.

"Loki! I thought maybe I imagined you."

"Maybe you did, but reality is overrated."

"Would you like a drink, Mr. Loki?"

"Yes, please."

Carrie poured him a dark beer. He took several large swallows.

"This is excellent."

"Thanks. It's my own recipe."

"Are you staying in town or just passing through?" John asked.

"I'm just catching up with my literary agent. Going to Tablerock to sleep on the beach and watch the sunrise. Then I'm going back to Europe. Got a promise to keep with some friends of mine, and a date with German apple pie. You ever have real German apple pie?"

Carrie and John shook their heads.

"Let me tell you, the recipe is handed down from mother to daughter for generations. Oh, the crust, the filling…I can taste it like a savored kiss."

"Sounds like you really like food."

"Not just food. This is art. This is unbelievable. If you could paint something as visually striking as that pie is flavorful, oh my god, that would be a masterpiece."

Loki's enthusiasm made Carrie giggle and John's stomach growl.

"I won't take up anymore of your time. Thanks for the beer, and oh, let me give you my latest book."

He handed them a book of poems called 'Our Night with Blue Stars'.

"This is a departure for me. I met this woman over there, and well, I'm a bit smitten. Have a good night."

Carrie called after him as he reached the door.

"What's her name?"

"Karen."

He disappeared as quickly as he had come in. John opened the book and read out loud to Carrie:

Our Night with Blue Stars

I have painted you a sky.
A sky held up by love,
a sky who breaks down weeping
with blue stars
on nights like this.

The sound of our lovemaking
carves itself upon Sea cliffs,
sinks into riverbeds,
is picked up by birdsong;
Nature shivers with pleasure.

You have kissed my naked shoulders,
they became great feathered wings
to lift you, to cool and protect you.

I am fascinated by your hands,
the way worlds take flight in them,
and in the music you play upon
my spine.

Nature seems to have shaped us
from the same red clay,
then dashed the design against her wall.

She said:
Let them wander,
and when they find each other,
rejoice.

ABOUT THE AUTHOR

T. Monroe has been published in various newspapers and anthologies, and served for several years as the President of the Saddleback College Poetry Club. He is also the author of the novel, Neeva's Gift, and releases music under the moniker "The Sky Catching Fire".

Made in the USA
Middletown, DE
08 February 2022